Warped Creatures

Perverted Science

Machines That Think

...And Hate...

Here are 8 high-voltage shockers that will stand your hair on end and chill the marrow of your bones.

L. Sprague de Camp and the other top writers warn you: *this is not a book for readers who have nightmares!*

Also Available

TWISTED

An unholy bible of weird tales by Ray Bradbury, Theodore Sturgeon and others. Edited by Groff Conklin

#L92-535, 50¢

THE WEIRD ONES

Unforgettable stories by the modern masters of science fiction.

Introduced by H. L. Gold

#L92-541, 50¢

See special-offer coupon on last page of this book

RARE
SCIENCE
FICTION

Edited by
IVAN HOWARD

BELMONT BOOKS • NEW YORK CITY

RARE SCIENCE FICTION contains eight prize-winning stories which have never been published in book form before.

BELMONT BOOKS

First Printing January 1963

BELMONT BOOKS / published by
Belmont Productions, Inc.
66 Leonard Street, New York 13, N. Y.

© *1954, 1955, 1957, 1959, Columbia Publications, Inc.*

PRINTED IN THE UNITED STATES OF AMERICA

CONTENTS

RARE SCIENCE FICTION

LET'S HAVE FUN

by L. Sprague de Camp

DOC LOFTING was on another drunk in the recreation room of the Embassy. This was different, being a crying drunk. The Fourth Secretary, Kemal Okmen, asked: "What's the matter, Doc?"

"Uzhegh dead," mumbled Lofting, a plump little man with a white goatee.

"The Provincial?"

"Yes."

"A friend of yours? I know you like these lizards—"

"Hadn't seen him in years."

"Then why the grief?"

"Reminds me . . ."

"Of what?"

Cecil Mpanza, the Communications Engineer, dropped into the third chair. "It's his big secret."

"What secret?" asked Okmen.

"Whatever brought him to Ahlia, twelve years ago; whatever made him stick despite heat, fog, and gravity. Whatever makes him do favors for the Ahlians."

"Isn't it time you told?" said Okmen.

Doc stared at his glass. "Well, now Uzhegh's dead . . ."

"Well?"

"Buy me 'nother and I'll tell."

"I take refuge in Allah!" said Okmen. "Charlie! Give Doc another. Now talk, old boy."

Doc wiped away the tears. "How to begin . . . Won't matter now. Too far in . . ."

"In what?" said Okmen.

"Confederated Planets. This thing—this—well, what

7

brought me here—was back in twenty-seven, when the first Interplanetary Conference was held."

"The one in the U.S.—the one that set up the C.P.?" asked Mpanza.

"Yes. I was jush—just a general practitioner in the suburb of Far Hills, near the Conference." As Lofting proceeded, he seemed to get the knots out of his tongue. "You've read about it. The old problem: local independence versus unity. The Ansonians refused to attend, and are still outside the Confederation; the Ghazaqs sent an unofficial observer, and joined later; the Ahlians sent a delegation, but all tied up with restrictions."

Mpanza asked: "Is that why the Confederation's constitution is so weak?"

"Partly. Lot of other delegations, including our own, were under similar restrictions. Most intelligent organisms like to order outsiders around, but are horrified by the idea of being ordered in their turn.

"Now, the Ahlians were a special case. They were barely willing to consider any agreement; if they were pushed, they'd pull out. Those who wanted a strong union wanted Ahlia in. It's a rich and powerful planet, and the Ahlians have a lot of what we unscientifically call character."

"All the stuffy virtues," said Okmen. "Thrift, punctuality . . ."

Back in twenty-seven, five youths stood in front of the post office in Far Hills' small shopping center. In age, they ranged from fifteen to nineteen. All were decently dressed in shorts and T-shirts; all looked well-fed and well cared-for. But they scowled. They scowled because Mr. Patchik had ordered them out for making a disturbance. So they had left the delightful coolth of Patchik's Drug Store to stand in the dank ninety-degree heat.

Their speech must be abridged because it consisted largely of Anglo-Saxon monosyllables, used with wearisome repetition. Bowdlerized, it ran as follows. Meehan, the oldest, said: "Let's have fun."

"Such as?" asked Fisher.

"I know a place we can drive two hundred miles an hour."

"Nah, they got a cop watching it. That's how Buddy Garstein got spattered last month."

"I seen it," said Carmichael. "Funniest thing you ever saw, poor Buddy spattered all over the county, from trying to get away from that cop."

Snow said: "Some day I'm gonna get that buggy cop. If you tie a herculite wire across the road on a level with his neck—"

"Nah," said Meehan. "They're conch to that one; that's why they got that cutter-bar in front of their windshields. What else you spuds got in mind?"

"I know a couple of girls we could get to come out in Smathers Park," said Carmichael. "There's a place low down with shrubbery around. If they yelled, nobody'd hear."

"Nah, I like mine willing," said Meehan. "How about a barn? Couple barns haven't been burned yet."

"Good idea," said Fisher. "I saw the Morrison barn get burned. Funniest thing you ever heard, way those horses screamed while they was roasted." Fisher giggled.

"Dunno," said Carmichael. "After these last fires, a lot of people are sitting out in their barns with shotguns. I got a better idea. You know old man Slye? He's got a marble statue in his garden—some kind of nymph or Venus or something. Old man Slye sure loves that statue. Well, let's bust it up; I can get a sledge-hammer."

"Hey," said Meehan. "Here comes Longpants Riegel with his tame lizard. One of those whatjacallems."

"Ahlians," said Kraus, the youngest.

The others gave Kraus a frosty stare; he had been guilty of knowledge.

"Like to get one of those buggy lizards," said Meehan. "Hang his head on my wall."

"You'd have a time," said Carmichael.

"Nah, with a good rifle? They wouldn't do nothing to me."

"How come they wouldn't?"

"They're not human, that's how come. The lizards."

"Maybe they got a closed season on 'em," said Kraus.

"So what? My old man would pay my fine. I'd just scream I was being frustrated. Some day we gotta give Longpants a visit."

"Yeah," said Snow. "Look at his buggy pants. And walking, in this weather; he's buggy, all right."

"Guess he's got to walk," said Kraus. "He couldn't get the lizard in his car. That lizard must be eight feet high."

"Playing around with off-earthers proves he's buggy," said Fisher.

Assistant Professor of Astromagnetics Norman Riegel was now within earshot, accompanied by Uzhegh of Kich. Uzhegh was the delegate to the Interplanetary Conference from the planet named by Terrans, after its human discoverer, Captain Hjalmar Ahl. The Ahlians called their own world Hwrajar—Pchum, but for obvious reasons earthmen preferred "Ahlia."

Riegel, dwarfed by his reptilian friend, had a few mildly-eccentric habits. For instance, he wore long trousers through the summer, instead of shorts, because he was conscious of his scrawny legs and varicose veins. He shaved the sides of his face in a decade when burnsides were universal.

As he neared, the five began muttering like ventriloquists without moving their lips:

"Look at the mad scientist!"

"Watch out, he'll bite."

"Look at his buggy pants."

"Lizard-lover!"

"Oh, Professor! *Whee-Whee-eew!*" he whistled.

Riegel marched ahead, his face set. He had to shoulder his way between Meehan and Carmichael to enter the post office.

"Look how mad he looks."

"Bet he'd like to kill us."

"Aw, he won't do nothing."

"He's too buggy to do anything."

Uzhegh remained outside, because the door was small for him. As Riegel came out with a handful of mail, the muttering rose again. Uzhegh leaned over and yawned suddenly in Fisher's face, showing his teeth and flicking out his long yellow tongue.

Fisher gave a little shriek, tried to leap back, tripped, and sat down. The other four youths laughed. While their attention was on Fisher, Riegel went into Patchik's Drug

Store. Here he picked up an afternoon paper and bought a gallon of ice-cream. Then he and Uzhegh set off towards the Scarron mansion, where Riegel and his wife lived while they ran the estate as a kind of camp or boarding-school for the young of the delegates to the Conference.

"Will thith not melt on ze way home?" asked Uzhegh, carrying the container.

"No; that's a new super-insulating plastic," said Riegel. "It'll keep for a week, even in this heat."

"Zat—that will be long enough for this party. Tell me, why did zose young Terrans treating you so disrespectful? Are they members of some hostile clan?"

Riegel shrugged. "No. They just don't like me."

"Why?"

"I suppose I know too much."

"That is a peculiar reason."

"Well, there's always been some hostility between the thinking fraction of my species and the unthinking majority. It becomes aggravated as science advances, and becomes less comprehensible to the layman."

"Why do you thubmit?"

"What could I do? I'm not allowed to shoot them. If I punched one, the rest would spatter me. At least two are bigger than I, and I'm three times their age. And if I beat up one, I'd go to jail."

"It is not the way we do sings," said Uzhegh. "Now, tell me, this is a working day, and zey look old enough to work. Why are they doing nossing?"

"Don't you know about our educational and child-labor laws? They're not allowed to work until they're twenty-five."

"Why? They looking adult."

The unions want 'em out of the labor-market. There's not enough work to go around even with our eighteen-hour work-week. So the state makes all the young stay in school till they're twenty-five. It's summer vacation now, but thank God that'll soon be over."

"I should sink all that education would make them more courteous and cultured-acting."

"Oh, most of them passed the academic saturation-point years ago—at thirteen or fourteen."

"The adademic what?"

"I mean, they're incapable of absorbing any more book-learning. They can't be taught trades, because their parents all want them to belong to the business and professional classes, and are outraged if they're made to use their hands. So they're given courses in things like basketry and square-dancing; between times they hang around, bored and spoiled, and think up deviltry."

"I am not sinking we should find this custom thuitable."

"You stick to your own customs. If any missionaries for Terran ideas come to Ahlia, I hope you kill them."

Uzhegh shook his crested head. "Yet you have an elaborate apparatus for enforcement of law. Why is it not operating?"

"Because of our theories of juvenile psychology. These hold that all misbehavior is the result of frustration or insecurity, and therefore the parents' fault."

"I am glad all Terrans are not like zose. It is partly knowing some like you and Doctor Lofting that made me recommend that our delegation be empowered to sign the constitution. You have done marvelous to keeping ze young of all those different thpecies playing together."

"It hasn't been easy," said Riegel. "Some are worse than human children. The young Akhran is careless about its respirator, and twice we've found it after it had taken it off and passed out. The Moorians, being arboreal, are almost impossible to housebreak. And I had to refuse admission to the young Ghazaq for fear it would eat some of our smaller off-earthers."

"Considering their ancestry, it is natural. How is my Tsitsav?"

"Fine."

"Has he behaving?"

"Very well; he's a responsible youngster."

"We of Hwrajar—Pchum all are, by comparison."

"Tsitsav has taken the Gordonian, Kranakiloa, under his wing."

"Wing?"

"Protection. Gordonians are jolly enough but carry playfulness to the point of damn foolishness."

"I know; they clown even in ze most solemn moments at the Conference."

They walked in silence. Riegel glanced with affection

towards the tall solemn Ahlian. He had found Ahlians the most attractive of the delegates, though most Terrans considered them stuffed-shirty. Their rigid morality struck most Earthmen as either hypocritical or impractical. At the same time it made the more flexible Terrans uncomfortable in their presence. Perhaps Norman Riegel liked them because he was a little like an Ahlian himself.

Uzhegh spoke: "Here we are. Where do I putting zis container?"

They were walking up the driveway of the Scarron estate. The estate had been for sale since Mrs. Scarron died at the ripe, but not exceptional age of 143. None of the heirs wanted the place to live in, as the mansion was considered a white elephant. When the Conference had begun, the Terran bureau that coped with other-worldly visitors sought a means of caring for their young. The bureau had therefore approached Riegel, as the local head of the Society for Interplanetary Union. He, in turn, persuaded the Scarron heirs to lend the mansion rent-free for the summer, and got a furniture-dealer to lend some second-hand furniture. Riegel and his wife, childless themselves, moved into the mansion and ran it as a school-camp for young off-earthers.

Now the Constitution was about to be signed, and the extraterrestrial young given back to their parents, the Riegels intended to give the young ones a last farewell party.

Somebody saw Riegel and Uzhegh. The twenty-three off-earthers poured out, walking, running, hopping, and slithering. The one that looked a little like an aard-vaark, for instance, was Gnish Axal, the Vza from Altair V. They talked in various approximations of English, except the Wanian, whose vocal organs did not work in the human aural range; the Thomasonian, who communicated by sign-language; and the two Borisovians, who talked by flashing built-in colored lights.

The Gordonian, Kranakiloa by name, flowed out with the rest. It looked something like an oversized otter with six limbs. The Gordonians presented a problem to the Conference. The had the lowest intelligence of any species represented, though they talked and used tools. There had been discussion of putting them under a trusteeship, but the delegates could not agree on any plan.

Kranakiloa danced around Riegel and Uzhegh, squeaking: "Gimme! Gimme!" and snatching at the container of ice-cream. Then Tsitsav, the young Ahlian, caught the Gordonian, shook it, and said: "Run off and play or I will thpank you."

Tsitsav was about as tall as Riegel, though of even lighter build. He spoke in his own language to Uzhegh, who responded. Their long forked tongues flicked out, touched, and vanished. Riegel had an impression that the older Ahlian was devoted to his offspring, but it was hard to tell. To an outsider, Ahlians' faces seemed expressionless.

The Ahlians walked off claw in claw. Alice Riegel came out and shooed the off-earthers back to their play-ground. She gave Riegel a sharp look and said: "What's the matter, darling?"

"Nothing. Just the young thugs at the post office." Riegel gave details.

"Shouldn't you tell the police?"

"That wouldn't do any good. I've told you before. They haven't done anything to be arrested for."

"Couldn't disorderly conduct be stretched to cover it?"

"It could be, perhaps but it won't. You know how people are. 'Nothing's too good for *our* kids'—and they won't believe what *'our* kids' are up to." A wild look came into Riegel's eye and a shrill hoarse tone into his voice. The effect was startling, as his manner was normally urbane and self-possessed. "Some day I'll get a gun and mow the little bustards down! King Herod had the right idea."

"Now, dear," said Alice Riegel. "You need a good strong cup of tea."

"What I need," said Riegel, "is a set of crosses, some spikes, and a hammer."

"The party's coming fine," said Alice brightly. "They've been as good as gold, except that Gnish started to dig up the front lawn for grubs; and I caught Kranakiloa dancing on the high-diving springboard. When I ordered him down, he just laughed."

"What did you do?"

"Oh, Tsitsav hauled him down and spanked him, though it's a little like spanking a piece of steel cable."

"They *are* tough. How about the pool?"

"We've drained and scrubbed it. Doctor Lofting's coming over to give them their final checkups and help with the party."

"Good old Doc! Without him and Tsitsav, I don't know how we'd have survived."

The five youths leaned against the front of the post office. Fisher, having picked himself up, glowered at the backs of Riegel and the Ahlian. He said: "Now we just gotta spatter those . . ." He rolled out a string of epithets that stigmatized his subjects' legitmacy, ancestry, chances of salvation, and sexual habits all at once. "We're not gonna let 'em get away with that!"

"What you got in mind, spud?" asked Meehan.

"Listen. Longpants bought a gallon of ice-cream. That means a party for all the little off-earthers, see? Now, have we all got baseball bats?"

"I don't have none," said Snow.

"Then we'll bust into old man Rizzi's sporting-goods store and get you one. Now, here's what we'll do . . ."

He was finishing his explanation when Doctor Lofting got out of his car and walked towards the post office. Again the ventriloquistic muttering arose:

"Look at old Whiskers."

"Bet he chews it in his sleep."

"Nah, that's to make him look like a doctor."

"Him a doctor? Just a drunken old bum."

"He couldn't doctor a horse."

At the entrance to the post office, Lofting turned and said pleasantly: "Boys, if you're trying to make a date with me, you're wasting your time. I'm not that kind of guy."

Then he went in. Lofting at this stage was neither old nor drunken; merely convivial and middle-aged. A widower, he had been drawn to the Riegels by a common interest in the Society for Interplanetary Union. His beard was the only unconventional thing about him, though it was enough to draw the attention of the five.

As Lofting got back in his automobile, Carmichael said: "Sassy little bustard, ain't he?"

"Some day we'll pay him a visit," said Snow.

"Hey, not till we've worked Riegel over!" said Fisher.

"Okay," said Meehan. "Time enough to figure something out for Doc later. Let's meet at twenty-hundred. . ."

The party went beautifully through the long August evening. The young off-earthers sang and romped and played games—all but Gnish the Vza, who lay panting in the heat, and the spidery Martian, who was not built for Terran gravity.

Alice Riegel looked at the darkening sky. The Gordonian was getting out of hand, prancing around and nipping the other guests to get them to chase it. Twice Norman Riegel had ordered it down from the high-diving tower of the empty pool.

Lightning flashed and thunder growled. Zeu, the Morenan, threw its tentacles around Alice Riegel in terror. She called: "Dear! We'd better take them inside."

Riegel looked skyward. "Not yet; it won't rain for another half-hour."

Meehan's gang watched the proceedings through a privet-hedge on the grounds. While Mrs. Scarron lived, her gardener had kept the hedge in trim; but now it had shot up to a height of ten feet. From where they stood, the youths could see the mob of young extraterrestrials playing behind the house—but not the kitchen door, which was hidden by a corner of the rambling edifice.

The gang had arrived late because Kraus had not appeared at the rendezous, and they had gone to fetch him. In fact, he was afraid of the consequences of the raid, and less avid for aggression and destruction than the others. He had hoped they would go without him. But when they appeared at his home, fear of losing status as a gang-member led him to join them.

"Shall we get 'em now?" whispered Fisher, swinging his bat in little circles. "Shall we?"

"Wait till it gets darker," said Meehan. "They'd know us, even with masks, in this light."

"Gonna rain soon," said Snow. "Then they'll go in."

"Keep your shirt on, spud," said Meehan. "Who's running this?"

"Boy, I'd sure like a crack at that Martian," said Carmichael. "He'd go splush like a bug."

"He's a buggy bug all right," said Snow, suppressing a giggle at his own wit.

The off-earthers played musical chairs, all but the Martian, the Vza, and Kranakiloa the Gordonian. Kranakiloa was chasing its tail in circles, as its mind could not be kept on any one thing for more than a few seconds.

Thunder came louder. Though the sun had not long set, the clouds darkened the scene almost to full nocturnal gloom. Doc Lofting, wearing a butler's apron, called from the kitchen door: "Hey, Norman! Better start herding 'em in. I'll dish up the ice-cream and cake." Those off-earthers who could not eat these substances were to get their native foods.

"We *gotta* go now!" wailed Fisher.

"Okay, put the bags on," said Meehan. Each youth produced a paper bag with holes cut for eyes, pulled it over his head, and fastened it in place with a rubber band around his neck.

"Hurry up!" groaned Fisher.

"Ready?" said Meehan. "Let's go!"

The Riegels were herding the last of the extraterrestrials in the kitchen door when the five youths pushed through the hedge, breaking down some of the privet-plants, and ran towards the back of the mansion. They ran quietly, stopping and gripping their bats. As they rounded the corner of the house they could see the kitchen door and the tail-end of the procession going in.

At that instant, Kranakiloa ducked under Riegel's arm and bolted out the door, screeching: "You gan't gatch me!" It loped across the back lawn towards the swimming-pool. The first drops fell.

"I will getting him, Profethor," said Tsitsav, the young Ahlian. He pushed past Riegel.

Kranakiloa headed for the high-diving tower. Fisher pointed at the long dark shape rippling past in front of the gang.

"Let's get that one!" he said. "He's by himself."

"Come back!" cried Tsitsav.

Kranakiloa glanced around. There was a bright flash

and a crash of thunder; Kranakiloa scooted for a patch of shrubbery.

"Hey! Who you are?" said Tsitsav to the gang as they converged from different directions on the track of the fleeing Gordonian. The gang slowed uncertainly. Tsitsav danced around to place himself between them and Kranakiloa, who had vanished into the bushes.

"You go away!" said Tsitsav. "I am responsible for him."

Meehan and Fisher stepped forward, swinging their clubs. Tsitsav advanced too, baring his teeth, though he weighed only half what they did.

There was an instant of furious whirling action, a thudding of bats in the hands of five brawny adolescents, and then they steped back. Meehan wrung blood from his right arm, which had been gashed by Tsitsav's teeth. Tsitsav lay on the sward, his limbs thrashing and tail flopping.

The sound of footsteps brought the boys around. Riegel and Lofting were bearing down on them, the latter armed with a rolling-pin. The Meehan gang, despite their advantage in weight and armament, raced off into the darkness, scattering. The older men ran after them until they were winded and the youths had outrun them and vanished.

"C'mon back—see if he's alive—" gasped Lofting.

He and Riegel returned, breathing heavily. The rain started to come down hard. Riegel said: "Did you see—any of their faces?"

"No—they had some kind of mask—or hood."

Riegel raised his voice over the storm. "I can guess who they were."

"So—can I but—you'd have a hell of a time proving it."

The got to where Tsitsav lay. Lofting bent over and said: "Get my bag. You'll find it inside the front door. And tell Alice to keep the others in."

When Riegel got back, Lofting looked up at him, water dripping from his goatee. "I'll check, but it'll just be a formality."

"Dead?"

"Good and dead. Skull smashed."

"Isn't there—I mean, he's more like a reptile, and they're pretty tenacious . . ."

"No. His brains are squashed and his heart's stopped." Lofting got instruments out of the bag.

"Shall I call police?"

"Just a minute. Let me think," said Lofting. He continued his examination. The downpour slackened.

At last Lofting spoke: "If we call the cops, they'll arrest our young friends and there'll be a big stink. But nobody'll be convicted. We can't swear we recognized anybody, because of those bags over their heads. Even if we could, you know what juries are. Electrocute one of our poor dear boys for socking some slimy reptile from outer space?"

"We have to start *somewhere* with equal enforcement of law."

"What law? The state legislature debated a bill to count off-earthers as people at the last session, but did nothing. Some politicians used just that argument about our poor dear boys. No doubt such a law will be passed, but not in time to help Tsitsav."

"Well, do we just let those little obscenities get away with it?"

"I'm thinking."

"What in hell shall I tell Uzhegh?"

Lofting continued: "If this comes out, it'll break up the Conference. The Ahlians won't sign the Constitution—not that I'd blame them—and a lot of the others will pull out too. Away goes interplanetary union! That's too important. I don't think it's worth revenge for Tsitsav's murder, even if we could get revenge."

"Well then, what? Shall we pretend it was an accident?"

"You're catching on, Norm. First I'll heave Tsitsav into the pool." The body flopped on to the concrete below. "Now let's catch that fool Gordonian. Maybe he doesn't know enough to spoil our scheme."

They dragged a whimpering Kranakiloa out of the bushes. The Gordonian could hardly talk intelligently—not that its talk was ever very intelligent. All they got from it was that it had seen Tsitsav running after it, had started for the shrubs, and then had been frightened out of its few wits by thunder and hidden itself.

"Go on in the house, Krana," said Riegel, "and get your ice-cream and cake." When the Gordonian had left, he said to the doctor: "It apparently never even saw the five masked figures. Now what?"

"We'll say Tsitsav climbed the tower, looking for Kranakiloa, and fell into the empty pool."

"So we did," said Lofting. "There was a lot of grief and sympathy but no hostility."

"But how did that land you here?" asked Mpanza.

"Couldn't stand it where I was. The Riegels got disgusted with Far Hills and moved away too. I stayed for a few years, watching Meehan's gang sneer when they saw me. They knew I knew. It hurt my professional conscience to fake the death-certificate; and it hurt it even more to let those five get away scot-free. Young Tsitsav, under his scales, was a *good* person.

"Well, I began hitting this stuff more than I should, and my practice went to pot. So I came out here, as it's hard to get a qualified medico to serve the Embassy on Ahlia. If you wonder why I like to do favors for the Ahlians, who aren't very chummy, it's to try to make things up to them."

Okmen said: "If the bottle bothers you, you can fix that by being psyched."

"But don't you see, their modern techniques drag everything out of you? How long could I have hidden the true story of Tsitsav?"

"Oh. But now—"

"Now I don't give a damn any more."

"Well, what did happen to Meehan's gang?"

"Oh, Meehan was killed in a knife-fight over a girl. Carmichael went to jail for burglary, and Fisher was killed trying to fly his family's plane under a bridge. The other two grew up to be more or less normal adults. A few years later, the current child-rearing fad changed from progressive-permissive to rigidly disciplinary. So, the last I heard, the kids were being kept under fair control. But from my point of view, the harm had been done. Charlie! Pour me another, please."

DO IT YOURSELF

by Milton Lesser

SEETHING, billowing fog greeted the rising sun as Robert McPeek shipped the oars of his dinghy and ran it aground on the east side of the river.

As much as McPeek hated the fog, he had to be grateful for it this once. With its help, he'd been able to lose the New Rochelle vigilantes in northern Manhattan. He wondered if they were still looking for him over by the North River, on the wrong side of the island. He shrugged. They were invading Manhattan territory and they knew it. If they hadn't already, they would have to give up the chase with the light of the new day. Besides, vigilantes distrusted one another and usually ended their pursuit in a senseless free-for-all. For the time being, at least, McPeek was safe.

He turned once and saw the upper half of the old U.N. Building—now the East Manhattan Home Workshop Center—rising ghost-like from the fog. Then he forgot all about the fog and the home workshop weather-makers who sowed their clouds from jerry-rigged planes, and dueled with artificial local high and low pressure areas like Cavaliers with swords—thus bringing the fog—and set out across the deserted wastelands of Long Island City, looking for work.

There was no work in Long Island City, of course. Someday in the future, the farms which had been moving east across the flat terrain of Long Island for a generation and more would encroach upon the gaunt, silent buildings and rat-infested rubble of Long Island City. Right now, though, the place was virtually deserted.

As the fog began to rise, leaving a last few tendrils on the ground to be dissipated by the rising sun, McPeek saw the scavengers, the homeless bags of rag, skin and bone who were the dregs of the old industrial society and hadn't yet been absorbed by the new rural America. They were pitiful creatures, looting what was left of the old abandoned warehouses. No one bothered them because no one else wanted the loot. Until the farmers moved as far west as the river, they were safe. Years or even decades, perhaps. Maybe it was better to be a scavenger, thought McPeek. His margin of safety might be measured in hours. Or minutes.

"Hello!" McPeek shouted as one of the scavengers, a grubby old woman in tattered cloak and shawl, came close. "I'm looking for Harry Crawford's farm."

The crone looked at McPeek from out of watery eyes, deep-sunk in folds of puckered skin. "Do which?" she croaked.

"The Crawford farm. It's right on the edge of Long Island City, I think."

"I don't have no truck with farmers." She looked as if she were waiting for McPeek to pull a weapon on her.

"I won't hurt you," he said. "You can save me a lot of time if you help me locate the farm. I'll pay you."

"Money? You can keep it."

McPeek had seen no money in two years. He shook his head, opened his traveling bag and withdrew a bolt of drab homespun he had received as partial payment on his New Rochelle job. "This," said McPeek. The material was drab but looked thick, felt heavy and might be warm. With winter coming, the crone eyed it greedily.

"Be a farm not two miles down the street, youngster. It's only one."

"You're sure?" McPeek said suspiciously. The crone could be making that up. Her eyes said she wanted the bolt of fabric, and two miles would be a long way for McPeek to come back running in case she had lied.

"That's the only farm I know of in this here area."

McPeek shrugged. He didn't need the bolt of homespun, except for barter. If the old woman were lying, he could chalk it up to overhead and find the Crawford farm on his own. He tossed her the bolt and watched her clutching at it with claw-like fingers, holding it close to her watery eyes and examining the warp and woof of the fabric. Satisfied, she hobbled away across the rubble, big black rats squeaking and fleeing from her path. She ignored them completely, but they unnerved McPeek. He set out for the Crawford farm, keeping to the middle of the cracked, weathered asphalt street.

A young man with a shotgun ready on the crook of his arm met McPeek at the gate of the Crawford enclosure. A nervous type, McPeek decided, tall and thin with an anxious harried look on his face and sinewy arms protruding from the short sleeves of the homespun shirt.

"What is it?" the young man growled.

"I'm looking for Harry Crawford."

"Is that so?"

"He's expecting me." McPeek reached into his pocket and got out a hand-printed card. He'd been right about the young man. The shotgun came down and pointed squarely at his chest until the young man saw it was only a business card he was fetching. The young man took the card, read it, then, following the instructions printed on it, lit a match and burned the card.

"This is the Crawford farm, isn't it?" McPeek asked, suddenly alarmed because the young man just stood there staring at him.

"Yeah. Yeah, sure. I never saw none of your kind before, that's all. I'm Gil Crawford, his oldest son."

McPeek sighed and relaxed. "Let's go on inside," he suggested. A moment later, Gil Crawford followed him inside the barbed wire enclosure.

A fantastic airplane of struts and wires and canvas—*and probably spit and string, too,* thought McPeek—skipped and sputtered through the air overhead. "My brother Paul's going up to sow some weather," Gil Crawford explained.

"Can he get enough altitude?"

Gil Crawford spat at his feet. "Got the plans in the Home Workshop Center. Took us two years to build. It ought to be good."

"I'm sorry," McPeek said. Maybe that was why he had never settled down on a farm of his own, he thought. You could make fun of a man's wife, or go to the other extreme and compromise her. You could laugh at his looks, or debate the fierce pride he took in his personal religion, or take liberties with his hospitality months on end. But criticize a product of his home workshop, and you had an enemy.

"There's Dad now," Gil Crawford said, pointing.

McPeek stared in that direction. The Crawford farmhouse was a small, one-story shack with sagging walls and unpaned windows. Evidently the Crawfords hadn't been here long. The house was always the last thing a man worked on.

Beyond the shabby house was a great sprawling structure of glass and cement block. Glass brick flanked the polished, ornate door in a decorative panel on either side. One of the Crawford family—it was usually a girl, McPeek knew—had painted murals on the cement block walls of the building. The murals had been executed with only a modicum of artistic talent but the labor which had gone into them must have been enormous. The murals depicted awkward, stick-like figures which McPeek assumed to be members of the Crawford family at work within the giant cement block structure, the workshop.

Striding out the door toward McPeek was a huge figure of a man, muscles bulging all over and threatening to force the seams of his homespun trousers, shirt and jacket. He had a surly, frustrated look on his face. His eyes were small, close-set, dogmatic. That was it, also, thought McPeek as Crawford approached. Dogmatism and a splintered, atomic, circumscribed and personal chauvanism. That was another reason why McPeek didn't fit; another reason why he was an outlaw.

"You must be McPeek," Crawford boomed. The voice fit the body, not the face.

"Pleased to meet you," McPeek said automatically.

"Well, I'm not pleased to meet you. Come on inside quick before some of the neighbors see you."

"Are they that close?" McPeek demanded, surprised.

"No, but they might be snooping. That's all we'd need, them catching one of your kind around here. Come inside, will you?"

At first McPeek thought they were going to lead him into the shabby house, but Crawford changed his mind and headed for the workshop. McPeek got one quick glimpse of the Crawford farm before he went inside. Most of the acreage was in weed. A few scrawny, ill-fed chickens were hopping about. A lean-to for the six or seven head of Crawford cattle had been slapped together on one wall of the rickety house, but McPeek thought better quarters would have to be provided for them by winter, which was not a long way off.

The workshop was different, as McPeek expected it would be. At one end of the cavernous l-shaped room McPeek saw the keel of a boat. It was far bigger than the dinghy he had stolen to flee across the East River from the New Rochelle vigilantes. It would be a cabin cruiser if Crawford could build an engine or find one— and then somehow get the gasoline to run it. Since the Crawford farm was a good two miles from the river, the boat—if and when completed—would have to be disassembled and carried down to the water piece by piece.

There was an unfinished tractor with all the latest Home Workshop do-dads.

There was the frame of an unfinished wagon, the wheel-spokes beautifully turned on the Crawford lathe.

There were parts of furniture, window frames (without glass), two ornate doors (minus hardware) which might be used in the Crawford house someday, picture frames, lamp bases (although McPeek had not seen a generator on the Crawford property,) a decorative pot-rack, window boxes and other things McPeek couldn't name. Stacks of Home Workshop plans and blueprints were piled on a table in one corner of the place.

"Sit down," Crawford said.

None of the furniture was finished, so McPeek sat on the floor in front of the unfinished boat.

"We found out about you from my cousin in New Rochelle," explained Crawford.

"I usually get my business that way. Word of mouth." It was the polite thing to say.

Crawford smiled. It was not a friendly smile. "Word of mouth, huh? We were snooping, McPeek. Plain snooping."

"That's none of my business."

"All right, this is. While you're here, you'll act like one of the family; can't have it any other way. If we get any visitors, which I doubt, *you're* my cousin from New Rochelle. Got it?"

"Yes," said McPeek.

"And let's get a few things straight. I don't like your kind. I never have and I never will. It's a shame, the kind of riff-raff an honest farmer has to associate with these days."

"You're right," McPeek said, "let's get a few things straight. I wouldn't be here unless you needed me. You know I can do the work because I come with family recommendations. But you're probably busy hatching schemes for what you're going to do after the work is finished. Just forget it."

"I ain't hatching no——"

"Well, if you are, forget it. You're afraid I'll talk. My kind doesn't; we survive on word of mouth good faith. But there are certain precautions which, naturally, I have to take."

"Such as?" asked Crawford belligerently.

"I've left the location of your farm, and your name, with my union. If I'm not back in Manhattan, safe, after a stipulated period of time, they'll make the knowledge public."

"They wouldn't!"

"Well, just see that nothing happens to me, that's all. You wouldn't want it known I've been working here. Sometimes you farmers figure the best way around something like that is to kill a man like me after he's finished. My union holds the information which says you won't."

"That's blackmail."

"I like it better than murder. Incidentally, we haven't discussed payment for my work."

"I got homespun the old lady does."

"Thank you, no. I'm not adverse to money; there are still some places you can spend it."

"We threw all our money away a long time ago."

"Jewelry, then?"

"We got some rings and things."

"Good. I'll take a look at them later. Right now I'd like to clean up and things if you don't mind."

"Got no privy," Crawford said. "I'm sorry about that. Been meaning to build one, but what with the boat and this furniture and all, I ain't had the time. There's a stream and a slit trench a couple of hundred feet south of the house."

"That will be all right," said McPeek. "By the way, do you have a master plan for the work you want done?"

"Haven't had the chance to draw one up."

"Well, I'll go over things with you after I clean up."

"How'd you like it?" Crawford suddenly asked, taking in the whole huge interior of the workshop with a sweeping motion of his arms.

"Nice," said McPeek diplomatically. "Of course, nothing is finished yet."

"Finished? Are you crazy? We're just getting started, ain't that right, Gil?"

The younger Crawford nodded.

We only been in it five-six years," his father went on earnestly. "Another five years, you wouldn't recognize this place."

"That's why I'm here," McPeek pointed out.

"All right. All right. Be quiet about that, will you? You don't have to rub it in. If you're going out to the stream, by the way, Gil will have to go with you. In case any of the neighbors are snooping. Nearest farm's only a mile and a half down the road. And you never know about those crazy scavengers. Lazy parasites. Won't do a lick of work for themselves."

"Let's go, Gil," McPeek said. He wished he was back in Manhattan already. Masochistic desire? He doubted it. Hiding from the law was better than this.

The Crawford farm, now five or six years in its present location, produced practically nothing. Crawford himself looked well-fed, but his wife was a scrawny woman who yawned constantly, and the six children, ranging from Mary, who was five, through Thomas, Jonathan, Hilda and the twenty-one year old twins, Gil and Paul, all looked undernourished.

McPeek had come into the kitchen unexpectedly. He watched the children, all but Gil who was still out at the slit trench, sitting apathetically at the table, and heard Crawford and his wife, who were out in the pantry, talking.

"Will you please hurry up?" Crawford said in a loud,

agitated whisper. "Git rid of those cans, for gawd's sake. You can't have him seeing cans in here; we're farmers."

"I'm doing the best I can, Harry."

Little Mary Crawford looked up at McPeek brightly and said, "Papa says you're the crook but we're to treat you nice."

"Shut up, will you?" teen-aged Hilda warned her younger sister.

"Yesterday I went into Long Island City on my first scavenger hunt and everything," Mary told McPeek.

"That's nice."

Hilda: "Shut up!"

"We found canned apergrass..."

"Asparagus," said Jonathan.

"And apple sauce and meat hash and all. Did you ever go scavenger hunting, Mr. Crook?"

"I'm afraid not," said McPeek. Hilda looked furious. "Your sister would rather you didn't talk, young lady."

"She made it all up about scavenger hunting," Hilda said. "We're farmers; we don't have to go grubbing around the city, do we?"

"Heck, no," said Thomas and Jonathan together. But Thomas, who was younger, winked at McPeek. "Are you going to tell us some vigilantes and crooks stories?" he wanted to know. "I never seen a real crook before. What do they do if they find you, put you in jail?"

Thomas must have been reading old books, thought McPeek. There were no prisons now; no organized law-enforcement—only the vigilantes, who banded together when necessary and did the job themselves, then as likely as not might be taking pot shots at one another for snooping. "No," McPeek said. "They'd probably chase me off Long Island."

Thomas looked disappointed.

"They sometimes might kill him," said Jonathan sagely. "Papa told me."

They might at that, McPeek thought grimly. Vigilantes were very unpredictable. With no specific code of law, there were too many variables, like what a man ate for breakfast and did he have an argument with his wife and how was the work coming in his workshop.

A few moments later, they sat down to a lunch of canned

asparagus, canned corned beef hash, canned plums and canned V-8 cocktail. All of it tasted exactly like canned food, but McPeek said nothing.

After lunch, McPeek inspected the farm with Crawford and drew up a tentative master plan. It would be a lot of work. A month, he thought. Maybe six weeks. It wasn't quite as bad as the New Rochelle job, thought McPeek. He had been there two and a half months.

Hardly looking at it, Crawford approved the master plan and went back to his workshop to putter.

Six weeks later, to the day, McPeek said, "Well, that's about all I can do."

"I don't like it," Crawford said.

"You don't like—?"

"No, not your work. I caught a couple of snoopers. Couldn't identify them. Gil and Paul had orders to shoot on sight, but they got away."

"I'll leave here tonight," McPeek decided. "I'll travel when it's dark. If they don't see me, they can't prove a thing."

Just then, the Crawford plane came soaring out of the sky and landed smoothly in the south field. "That sure is better," Crawford admitted. "There's so much to do, I don't have the time. You know how it is."

"Then you're satisfied with the work?"

"What I seen of it. I been busy, McPeek; I started another boat, by the way."

"Another one?"

"Well, it's a big family I got. If I finished one without the other, there'd be a lot of hard feelings. Also, they had a real bargain on blueprints over to the Home Workshop Center. A man can't resist a bargain, you ought to know that."

McPeek nodded, and received two rings and a jeweled bracelet as payment for his work. They'd bring a good price in Manhattan, either in money or bartered goods. Maybe he would take money this time, McPeek thought. It was time he left this part of the country, anyway. And money was still worth something up north in conservative Boston.

"I've got some farm now," Crawford was saying. "Maybe in the spring I'll even find the time to plant some crops. We should get the first snow soon, though, so I don't have to worry about planting till next year. There's a million things I've got to do in my workshop."

In six weeks, McPeek had managed to put the Crawford homestead in order. He had repaired the chimney flu, from which smoke was rising in cheerful lazy tendrils now. He had built a privy near the house, caulked and water-proofed the leaking roof, constructed a barn for the Crawford cattle, made a few major repairs on the weather-plane, constructed plywood windows which would keep out the snow, completed the work on Crawford's tractor in case the man could find some gasoline and ever got around to farming, and done a dozen or so other things around the place.

Naturally, if all went well, Crawford would be able to brag about the work as his own, provided he got any visitors, which was doubtful. Maybe, after a time, Crawford would talk it into himself and stomp back and forth proudly across his farm, convinced that, with slight help from his family, he had done the work.

McPeek shrugged. He didn't care. He'd been paid. The system was self-perpetuating now, and men like McPeek were necessary, but outlaws and—what was the word? —pariahs.

It starts with a war, McPeek thought, remembering the union booklet on the subject. Once unions weren't out-lawed organizations, but that was a long time ago. A war in which men learn skilled trades in the service of their country, and women take their places in the factories and on the assembly lines and learn they can use their hands for more than darning socks or cleaning house.

After the war—political isolation. A depression tossed in. People do things for themselves, before the depression because they have leisure time and are proud of their new-found skills, after the depression because they don't have money to pay for outside work. They begin to distrust outsiders; their homespun work is better. Capital and industry are artificial contrivances to keep a man in debt, anyhow.

Do it yourself, brother.

But with a new generation, the war-learned skills fade. It isn't a question of getting the people back to the farms, the union booklet said. Getting them back to the factories has become impossible. You work without pride on an assembly line. You put this bolt here or maybe slam down the drill press like so, but you don't even get to see the finished product.

A man has got to have pride in his work. Homespun, he does. Of course, the work isn't always practical. A man gets to dream around his workshop and does the work he likes best and is too busy for unimportant things like— well, like privies. That being the case . . .

"What did you say, Mr. Crawford?"

"It looks like trouble."

Little Mary Crawford came running toward them, her eyes brimming with tears. "I didn't want to tell," she cried. "I didn't want to, honest. They made me."

"Snoopers?" Crawford asked.

" 'Noopers, papa!"

"What did you tell them?"

"They made me tell."

"What, child?"

"We had a crook working here."

McPeek was already running for his traveling bag, tossing his gear in it. He heard shotgun fire from beyond the enclosure. "That's Gil and Paul," Crawford said breathlessly. "They know what it would mean for you to be caught here. Get lost, will you?"

"I'm going," McPeek said, taking a pistol from his bag before he closed it, and hoping he wouldn't have to use it.

"If you can get away, them snoopers can't prove a thing."

"Is there a back way out?"

"Over the fence. Hurry up!"

Jonathan sprinted up. "It's more than snoopers, papa; it's vigilantes."

"How do you know that?" Crawford asked.

"On account of there's ten of 'em. Who ever heard of ten snoopers together?"

McPeek and Crawford were running toward the rear line of the Crawford property. McPeek carrying his bag in one hand and his pistol in the other.

"Once I'm in open country I'll get away," he predicted.

"You're quick, huh?"

"I've got to be quick in my business."

"Here we are now," Crawford panted. The fence was four feet high, tight-stranded barbed wire.

McPeek fumbled through his bag for a pair of wire cutters. He began to snip the barbed wire with it. "The same thing happened in New Rochelle," he said. "Vigilantes."

"You got away?" Crawford's face was drawn and worried.

"I'm here, aren't I?"

It was growing dark now. McPeek looked up at the sky. A sullen blanket of clouds brooded there, low and laden. It was cold enough to snow. The darkness and the snow would be his best protection. But he was running again. He was always running. His kind was the most necessary single feature of the new slapdash agrarian society, but was outlawed. Someday men would learn, he thought.

McPeek's wire-cutter snipped through the last of the barbed wire. "Here," he said, giving Crawford a card. "Read it, memorize the address of my union in case any of your relatives ever need any work done, then burn it."

"Burn it, huh?" Crawford said speculatively.

"You've got to, for our protection as well as yours. If you're found with that card on you, it means you were in contact with one of us, doesn't it?"

"Well, yeah."

"Then read it—and burn it."

Crawford nodded. There was a commotion in the direction of the farmhouse. Several figures stumbled across the uncultivated land. A shotgun roared, the muzzle blast a fierce orange blossom against the gathering night.

"Get going!" Crawford pleaded.

McPeek went down on one knee and carefully aimed his pistol at the nearest figure. When McPeek fired, the man screamed, threw his shotgun away, and held his injured forearm. Then McPeek was gone swiftly in the dim twilight.

Crawford looked after him just once. He sure could melt off into the landscape, that guy. When Crawford turned back to look again, McPeek had vanished. He would get away, all right.

Quickly, before the vigilantes could reach him, Crawford read the business card and burned it. The card said:

BURN THIS CARD AFTER YOU READ IT! ! !
Robert A. McPeek
Manhattan Union 15
Times Square, New York
HANDYMAN

IN HUMAN HANDS

by Algis Budrys

THE CAPTAIN pointed out to his executive, "It's only one robot."

"I wasn't thinking of the harm in terms of property loss," the second-in-command answered. "Suppose he's *not* permanently disabled, somewhere. There are a dozen possible reasons for his not returning." He stared out through the ports at the mass of green and brown vegetation standing to all sides of the charred clearing where the three hulls rested. "I don't like leaving him."

The captain grunted. "That's a chance we'll take; we can't delay any longer." He rattled the paper bearing the transcribed sub-space radio message. "We've got to get back home. Besides, this's probably an uninhabited planet."

"We don't know that as a certainty," the exec answered.

The captain scowled impatiently. "What could one robot do, in any case?"

BEGINNING:

THE ROBOT smashed through a nest of creepers and interlaced vines, further damaging the buggy-whip antenna at the side of his head, but not stopping his precipitous run. He broke out into the edge of the clearing, and then stopped dead suddenly, his purpose lost as he watched the three Earth ships ladder up into the overcast. They punched through the clouds, sending doughnuts of vapor billowing away across the sky, and disappeared, the throaty grunt of their exhausts gradually dwindling.

And so, the robot was marooned; some scores of light

34

years away from the Earth and the culture of which he was now the sole representative on this planet. It was not until he had beaten his way out of the jungle, and into a moderately temperate zone, that he discovered the village in a curve of the shoreline along a broad and quiescent sea.

Tyrrel Cye awoke, rolled off his sleeping mat, and padded barefoot across the room to the washstand, where he buried his face in the water.

Running his wet fingers through his hair, he went over to the stone slab on which he had laid a fire the previous night, took the flint and iron from a peg in the ventilation hood, and set the tinder alight. He filled a pottery bowl with water, hung it over the fire, then walked back to pick up his wraparound.

As he was going by the door, Tyrrel looked out into the village square and saw the robot standing there, his head swiveling as he inspected the buildings.

Tyrrel frowned, stopped for a moment to get a more comprehensive look, then went to the clothes-rack, put on his wraparound, pulled the water pot off the fire, and went outside.

He walked a little carefully, but he had already decided that whatever kind of thing the robot might be, it was definitely displaying intelligent interest.

And intelligence, of course, indicated a lack of combativeness.

The robot turned his head to watch him come. Tyrrel noted that the glossy figure remained motionless, hands dangling open. He raised his own hands, palms forward to show that he was also unarmed; he was only partially surprised to see the robot make a head movement of understanding in reply.

Tyrrel decided to try speech. He stopped a few feet away from the robot and looked up at the expressionless face. "Welcome. I am Tyrrel Cye," he said, and waited for some answer from the robot.

The metal figure shook his head, then squatted down and ran an extended finger through the dust at his feet.

Tyrrel bent over to look at what he was doing. The robot was tracing dots and circles in the dust. He pointed up to the sun and then back down to a fairly large dot.

Tyrrel nodded. The dot represented the sun. The robot saw his nod, and nodded in return. Tyrrel remembered that the robot had shaken his head to indicate that speech was not a feasible communications medium as yet. "Well, at least we can say 'yes' and 'no' to each other," Tyrrel remarked.

The robot looked up. He pointed to his head and nodded in an exaggerated manner. Tyrrel frowned slightly, not sure of what the robot wanted, but nodded back in return. The robot shook his head violently, then nodded carefully once again. This time, Tyrrel understood; with equal care, he nodded back, and said "Yes" at the same time.

The robot nodded enthusiastically, and a perfect imitation of Tyrrel's voice said "Yes" from a grille in the upper part of his chest.

Tyrrel and the robot then launched into full-scale experiments in communications; and it was not until the robot had acquired a hundred-word vocabulary, and Tyrrel had picked up a smattering of Copernican astronomy in the course of learning that the robot came from another solar system, that they looked up and saw they were surrounded by a ring of villagers.

Tyrrel looked at his shadow; it was nearly noon. "Come on, fellow," he said to the robot. "It's time Kes Lorri got a look at you."

The robot had at least gotten the sense of Tyrrel's statement; he nodded and began to follow him through the crowd.

"It seems there are other worlds," Tyrrel said to an acquaintance in the crowd, "with people living on them who can travel from one to another. I can't quite make out whether this fellow's one of them or not. Anyway, we're going to see the Gansha; he'll probably hold a meeting when we find out a few more things. All right?"

"Sure."

"That shiny stuff he's got on is metal. But he isn't wearing it—it's him."

The villager shrugged casually, and stepped aside. The robot fell into step with Tyrrel, and they walked up the street to the Gansha's home.

II

It was evening before Kes Lorri and Tyrrel had learned as much of the robot's story as they could. Now the two men sat in silence while the robot waited on the open porch outside the Gansha's house.

As always when he called on Lorri, Tyrrel found himself studying the set of the silver-haired head on the tired shoulders, the occasional contraction of thin fingers on the edge of the old man's chair as a spasm of pain rippled through his body.

There would have to be an election soon, Tyrrel thought. Lorri was still the wisest man in the village, but there were others who could balance inexperience with the physical ability to carry out broader programs.

Coupled with the thought was the certain knowledge that he was the logical candidate to take the old Gansha's place.

He was half-afraid of the realization. The villagers were accustomed to the calm, deliberate counsel of experience —experience that stretched back to the time of the village's founding. If a young man became Gansha, then the village would have to fall back on trial-and-error. Would the villagers be satisfied with that, after the almost error-less guidance which Lorri had given them? And what would happen to the village if they were not?

What of the robot? How serious was the crisis he represented? He had come into the village this morning, and now the people of the village—the planet, Tyrrel corrected himself on the basis of his newly-acquired cosmology—knew that there were other worlds, other solar systems, and other men, all of which could come crashing down on the village at any time with overwhelming power.

Lorri broke the silence. "What do you think, Ty?" he asked.

Tyrrel frowned. "I don't know. There's too much to assimilate. Think of it!—infinities of circling globes around infinities of suns—the sheer cubic volume! And a culture that builds intelligence!

"We don't even know why he was abandoned; he doesn't know himself. There must have been some emergency, either aboard the ships or back home. But what? When are they coming back? Nobody can know that, either. What will happen when they do?"

Lorri said slowly, "It is a series of dependent riddles —and we have no answers except those we can imply from the questions themselves."

The old man shifted his position a little, and an expression of pain flickered across the lined face. "I'm afraid much of that will be left for you to deal with, Tyrrel," he said, his voice riding the gasp it could not cover. "But there are certain things that must go on, up to the very time the Earthmen come back."

"Are you sure they will come back?"

"If they came here once, they will return. Intelligent life does not retrogress; it cannot retrogress, or it betrays its own greatness. That is why we must continue as we have. We cannot plan on the return of the Earthmen as anything but another incident in our history, a brush with the rest of the universe, nothing more. We have to go our own way. We have no idea of what the Earthmen are like. They may have six tentacles and multi-faceted eyes, for all we know. Their civilization couldn't possibly fit us as well as our own can."

"What are we going to do about the robot?" Tyrrel asked.

"We'll have to know more about him before we can decide that. I'll leave that to you."

Tyrrel nodded. "He can stay at my house as well as he can at any other. He's learning our language rapidly —we'll be able to talk in fairly complicated sentences very soon, I think."

"All right." The old man looked around the room. "I think that's all we can do, for the present. Will you help me to my bed?"

Walking slowly, they crossed the room to Lorri's mat, where the old man sat down with a sigh. "Thank you," he said. He stretched out and looked up at Tyrrel, his eyes in shadow.

"I wish I were stronger," he said; "I wish I had years enough to see what our village will be."

He reached up and took Tyrrel's hand in his own. "A man always wishes for things, Tyrrel. When he grows old, he knows how many wishes he will never see fulfilled. But he knows, too, that the wishing—not the attainment —is the basis of civilization, and of learning. For, even if a wish is fulfilled, there are always new wishes, and as long as man keeps wishing—as long as men keep wishing, and trying—then life moves.

"There is no good in hoping that everything will be attained. Life is not so arranged."

Kes Lorri sighed again. "Goodnight, Tyrrel."

"Goodnight, Gansha Lorri," Tyrrel replied quietly, and walked softly across the room to the porch where the robot was waiting with machined patience.

III

While Tyrrel slept, the robot sat motionless in the darkness of his house. Most of his attention was devoted to an analysis of the information he had acquired during the day.

He felt no emotion. A man would have been incredulous and startled, the robot knew, for he was aware of emotion as a measurable abstract.

This village was primitive, true—but not ignorant. The villagers were humanoid—but inhuman, or, perhaps, superhuman, in the manner in which they were aware of their future course toward civilization. The very fact that they could conceive of such a thing, and be aware of their own lack of it, was unprecedented.

For example, they used crude meteoric iron. They knew about iron ore, and had reasoned out the process of smelting, but didn't bother. Tyrrel had pointed out, in answer to the robot's question, that iron was unsatisfactory in many respects. They were waiting, he had told the robot, until they found out how to modify it into forms more suitable for machinery.

The robot shook his head in the acquired Terrestrial mannerism. This was a young, vigorous civilization—and inhuman or not, its potentialities were staggering. And yet . . . Only Tyrrel had really displayed any great curiosity about him. The other villagers had been content to stand about idly, both while he and Tyrrel established communication, and later when the headman—the Gansha, Lorri—had told them what Tyrrel had learned about their extraordinary visitor.

Odd. He had always thought that curiosity was a prerequisite to intelligence. And Lorri—what of him?

The robot knew full well that human beings who asked no questions, and let subordinates convey information, were wary of the answers their own questions might imply. But Lorri was not a human being; still, he was intelligent, and logic was universal with intelligences of all sorts, was it not?

The robot nodded to himself in the darkness. Perhaps, tomorrow, he'd tell them about steel. But he'd have to be careful.

The village straddled the river, forming a cluster of houses to either side of the delta. At the river's mouth, light wharves ran out into the bay, and small sailing vessels were anchored near them.

The robot and Tyrrel stood on the hill that rose to one side of the river and surveyed the scene. "This is the only village on the planet, then?" he asked.

"That's right," Tyrrel answered. "There are about a thousand of us, I think. Our ancestors were a small band that moved out of the jungle and settled here. There may be others like them still in the jungles—or, perhaps, there may be offshoots like ours on the other side of the equator—but we don't know about them."

"And the village began functioning as a civilized community only about a hundred years ago?"

"Lorri became Gansha at about that time, yes; he deserves most of the credit."

"But he could never have brought the village up to this level singlehanded," the robot said. "There must have been others to help."

"Of course," Tyrrel agreed. "We're not all equally intelligent, true, but how can there be any opposition to progress? Most of the things we're trying to achieve in this generation are obvious necessities—things like a transportation network to provide us with foods that grow best in more distant places, and with supplies unavailable here. There should be a need for various minerals and fuel sources, once we start constructing machinery. We're working on communications, too. It's well and good to raise grain in a suitable climate—it's not so good to be out of touch with the harvesters for three months."

The robot nodded. "In other words, under the leadership of Lorri—though 'advice' would be a better word, I suppose—it's taken the village about a hundred years to change over from a huddle of fishermen's huts to the nucleus of a civilization which is about to enter an industrial period."

"That's right." Tyrrel stood beside the robot and looked out over the village. "I imagine it compares rather badly with Earth," he said, unable to keep from trying to find out. He recognized the feeling of weakness and inferiority the attempt implied, and his conscience felt no better for it. Still, he was human, Gansha-to-be or no.

The robot, for some reason, did not answer immediately, but continued to look out at the bay. His head moved as he followed the passage of a catamaran loaded with supplies for the grain colony—actually a small group of men living in one temporary building—that lay up the coast.

"You're a long way from interstellar travel," the robot said finally.

And what is that supposed to mean? Tyrrel thought, but he didn't press the point. There was time enough. Even this one week since the robot walked into the village had brought great progress to his visualization of what the future course of the village's history would have to be.

As they walked down the side of the hill toward the village, Tyrrel found himself studying the robot, watching the delicately-balanced shift of knee joints and ankles, the fluid slip of hips as the metal man strode.

"There must be a lot of similarity between ourselves and Earthmen, I imagine," he said.

"Quite a bit," the robot agreed. "The planetary ecology is about the same. The year is somewhat longer on Earth, but this planet was picked for its resemblances, of course."

That seemed to be all he was going to say on the subject, Tyrrel noted. The robot was obviously not too eager to discuss Earth and Earthmen, but he undoubtedly had some good reason.

The robot was a problem, however. In the past week, a dozen small groups had begun collating the various

sciences the robot had mentioned casually, and then out-
lined comprehensively when Tyrrel asked him to amplify.
It had already been necessary to expand the language by
half again.

Which was good. Lorri had approved, and reminded
Tyrrel that so long as the robot merely spared them basic
research, and did not delineate a firm line of approach
that could not help but be basically Terrestrial, the villagers would be free to develop basic applications of their
own, better suited to their own culture.

Still, the robot was a puzzle, for there was no apparent
good reason for him to be so cooperative.

Tyrrel smiled at himself. Undoubtedly, there was one,
and it would be discovered in time.

Yes, he thought suddenly, time . . . If the Earthmen
stayed away.

IV

A man stopped them at the edge of the village, and
Tyrrel frowned. The villager looked worried. "What's
wrong, Sern?" he asked.

"I'm not sure. Have you seen Kes Lorri today?" the
man suddenly blurted out.

"No, I haven't," Tyrrel answered. "The robot and I
went out right after breakfast." *It's come,* the thought
drove into him. He fought to keep his face calm. *And
I'm not ready.*

"I was over at my cousin's house all morning," Sern
explained. "You know—right across from the Gansha's
house. I noticed he wasn't out on the porch. He's always
out on the porch." Sern stopped, confused. "Isn't he? I
mean— I think so. I seem to remember. . ." He stopped
again, and mumbled down at his toes. "I guess it isn't
anything important; I wouldn't have mentioned it if I
hadn't bumped into you. Sorry I bothered you."

"Wasn't anything," Tyrrel said as casually as he could.
"It's probably nothing, but I'll check anyway. Thanks."

"All right." The man was obviously relieved, and continued on his way to the river.

Tyrrel's teeth nudged his lower lip. Lorri had never

said so, but wasn't it true that the villagers only carried their initiative so far, and then stopped?

But there wasn't time to stand there thinking brand-new thoughts. He motioned to the robot, and they walked rapidly toward Lorri's house.

Tyrrel's footsteps seemed to be impeded as they neared it. The functioning of his muscles was forced, rather than spontaneous. He realized suddenly that he was afraid of what he might find.

And what's suddenly gone wrong with me? he asked himself, the voice sharp in his mind. But he knew what was wrong. He was loosing the firm support of the old Gansha's presence.

Lorri had dragged his mat into the farthest corner of his house. In reflex, he had crowded himself against the woven grass of the wall and lay on his side, his head thrown back, his mouth strained open, his knees as high as his hips, his arms stretched limply out behind his back. His hands twitched at every painful breath.

Tyrrel's shadow fell into the house through the open doorway. "I think you'd better stay out here," he told the robot through his gathering numbness.

"He won't mind if I come in," the robot said firmly.

Tyrrel was too taken up to argue. He simply crossed the room with gentle footsteps, half-hearing the robot's equally gentle tread behind him. He reached Lorri's side.

The old man twisted his head, his eyes turning up toward the two; the robot quietly stepped back out of his line of vision.

"Tyrrel," the old man said. His voice blew out of his mouth like a shutter torn loose in a high wind. "Intelligent life does not retrogress. Remember. Retro—retrogression is a sign of failing intelligence. The village must rise. Heritage. *My* heritage. Took—took them out of the jungle. Came out of jungle when I dragged them—but they brought jungle with them. Led them out of it. Took a group of fish—fishermen. Made human beings out of them. I was only one saw—saw the way. Saw future— *I saw the future, Tyrrel!* In my mind—no mind ev' like it before. Saw how civi—civilization has to work. Interdependence. Figured out concept of interdepen'ce. Broad front of progress. Only a thousan' of 'em. Whole planet

to draw resources from. Not hard—small group. All believed in me. Followed advice. Good at that. Not resis—
resistant to information. Give 'em outline, they'll work,
fill in details. But got to give outline. No curiosity. Won't
look for things—but show 'em, and they'll carry on, long
as you keep pushing."

The old man suddenly twisted, interrupting the flow of
babbling that Tyrrel only half understood. One hand
reached up and closed on Tyrrel's wrist.

"You're nex' Gansha. Been building you up. Not smart
—not like me. Too much 'fluence from mother—" He
stopped suddenly, his eyes opening wide, as though he
had let something slip. Then he twisted his mouth in a
travesty of an ironic grin. "Won' understand anyway, will
you? Words of all-wise Gansha sometimes incompre—
prehensible, eh? Maybe you're mother's husban's son,
'nyway. But training—training counts, too.

"Keep pushing them, Tyrrel. Gave you broad outline,
how things have to go. Pass on to others. Don' let it end,
Ty. Have to civilize. Dirty, stinkin' fishing village. Hated
it. Built it up. Gonna go farther. They'll forget village,
build up into big culture, remember me. Always remember Gansha Lorri. Forget kid was too good to gut fish."

The Gansha's hand clenched convulsively on Tyrrel's
wrist. "Retrogression is a sign of failing intelligence," he
said with sudden clarity. "I never let them know how
sick I was. Don't let anybody in here; I don't want them
to see me. Tell them when I die; tell them I died in my
sleep. Stay here. Don't let anybody in, understand?"

The staring whites of Lorri's eyes dug at Tyrrel's face.
Tyrrel almost mentioned the presence of the robot, but
the old man went on, cutting him off before he could
do more than part his lips.

"Understand me, boy?" he said sharply. "Don't let
them come in and see me!"

Tyrrel nodded, and the old man grinned. He half-
raised his hand, then let it slide from Tyrrel's wrist to
fall to the floor beside him. He thrashed his body over on
its back. His eyes dropped shut, and his limbs shook in
spasmodic contractions at the pain that was tearing
through him; but he moved them slowly until they fell
into a rough approximation of a relaxed, peaceful attitude.

He lay on his back, his wracked face upward, his arms and legs jerking, but he had determined to die as though in peace. His breathing became convulsive, but did not stop as yet.

Tyrrel squatted down beside him, facing the door, his eyes clouded. He felt the numbness that had been encircling his mind steadily, that was now closing into a clenched fist of grief and loss. Through the numbness came a realization of how great a man Kes Lorri had been. How his thoughts and energies had always been directed toward the progress of his people, until, even now, delirious and half-babbling with pain, he had nevertheless gathered his last dregs of determination and passed the torch on to his hand-picked successor.

And then the fist closed around that thought, and around the pain and desolation. It left him squatting beside the Gansha, filling his mind while the old man slowly died.

V

The robot looked at the two humans from his shadowed corner. The answer to the riddle of the village had finally come.

He'd been given false data—or, perhaps, rephrase to "insufficient data." The village civilization was not spontaneous, the product of steady evolution; rather, it had risen artificially on the momentum of one man's ambition. A paranoid, but a genius. Perhaps the qualities were interrelated; the robot had never completed his data files on psychology.

The robot, of course, was incapable of the physiological expressions of irony. He could, however, chuckle in his mind. So the old bachelor had tried to keep the genius strain alive, eh? Well, he had failed here, but it might turn up again . . . if Tyrrel had a child, say. And if one man had it, might there not be others?

The robot did not, as yet, know what he was going to do about that.

Tyrrel was a problem. The old man had woven well, but the son was never going to be able to hold the complex program together.

What to do? The robot integrated his data, and arrived at the obvious solution—a solution so good that it fitted in perfectly with the robot's own motives; now he knew what his next course of action must be.

He had arrived at his conclusion with no time to spare. The Gansha's breath whistled out between his teeth. The shaken body slumped into relaxation. The old man's last wish had been granted.

The robot padded gently past Tyrrel and closed the staring eyes. He raised the dropped jaw, and turned the head so that it would not fall again.

"His pain has stopped," the robot said.

Tyrrel raised his eyes and saw the robot looking at him across Kes Lorri's body. "You will be voted the next Gansha," the robot said.

Tyrrel nodded woodenly. The functioning of his mind was hampered by the stricture of grief, yet, the very fact that they had stood this death-watch together, or else some other mysterious kinship, was enough to make less of an alien and more of a fellow out of the robot.

"Do you think you're too young?" the robot asked.

Tyrrel felt his eyes widen with surprise. "I don't know," he answered. "It's hard to judge your own experience; I'm still not used to the thought that a judgment is necessary."

The robot nodded, and Tyrrel startled himself even more by realizing that it was a nod of agreement.

"I know," the robot said.

He knew? How could he know? But, somehow, Tyrrel felt that he did. Almost as though the robot were partially filling the emptiness that Lorri's death had left, he could feel the numbness begin to drain from his mind, leaving the sorrow but taking away the paralyzing grief.

"I'll have to let the villagers know," he said. He stood up and began to walk out of the house.

"What about the body?" the robot asked.

"He had no family," Tyrrel answered. "I'll burn the house tonight."

The typical barbarian funeral, the robot thought. *I'll change that in you yet, Gansha Cye.*

VI

Tyrrel looked down from his doorway at the gathered villagers. Every face reflected the same numbed irresolution he himself now felt to a lesser degree.

"We'll have to hold an election as soon as possible," he said heavily.

One of the men in the crowd raised his head. "If it's all right, I don't see any need for one. We all know the Gansha wanted you to follow him; we've all learned that the Gansha always worked and planned for the good of all of us. So I don't see why we shouldn't just call you—" —the man's unaccustomed tongue stumbled over the words—"Gansha Cye."

The rest of the crowd murmured in affirmation.

Tyrrel felt his eyes welling over; his throat filled with a warm lump that he swallowed jerkily. "Thank you," he said haltingly, and then, at the comprehension of his inheritance, he turned quickly and got inside the house, his steps uneven.

The robot was waiting for him. "I heard them," he said, his calm voice bringing a measure of relaxation to Tyrrel's overstrained nerves. "It's a big responsibility, isn't it?"

Tyrrel nodded silently.

"It's not as big as it seems right now," the robot said gently. "Kes Lorri left the program mapped out behind him; he was a wise man. If you follow his plan, you and your people will rise to the heights he dreamed of."

"You'll help me, won't you?" Tyrrel suddenly found himself saying, and immediately knowing that it was what he had been *wanting* to say since Lorri's death.

The robot nodded. "I'll be glad to tell you about the various fields of scientific investigation. My data-banks, of course, contain the sum total of all the universal natural laws which have been discovered on Earth, and I'll be glad to supply you with those.

"I understand, quite well, that every culture must do things its own way—that every type of intelligence has its own motivations, and their concommitant expressions.

But Lorri has already laid down the plan of your progress, so that there is no danger of contamination.

"You see what we can do? We can short-cut all along the line, for technological evolution is only a process, not a necessity. Why bother with coal, when you're free to begin with atomics, a point which took the Earthmen centuries to reach? But I won't tell you how to build atomic reactors— I'll simply supply you with the working principles, and you can develop your own, applying them where they best seem required for your culture.

"I won't tell you how to build a spaceship, but I'll give you the laws of nuclear physics and astronautics— how you make use of them is something that will have to spring from your own cultural background."

"You know," Tyrrel said, "that's almost what Lorri told me, the first night you came here."

"Is it?" The robot paused for a moment, and then went on. "You see? It's what Lorri planned. Once you have industry, of course, the village will grow into a city. It will stay that way for a while, and then, as your population rises, your people will scatter out over the world, until, actually, you have a decentralized culture, with the city remaining as the central point from which the power and commodities flow. By then, you'll have a communications net all ready to handle the job.

"After that, furthur expansion, into the stars."

Into the stars, Tyrrel thought. On common ground with the Earthmen, and a civilization too well established to be warped or contaminated. In fact, the shoe would be on the other foot. It would be the Earthmen who would have to be wary.

As the robot talked, unfolding his plan—so parallel to Lorri's own—all the obstacles which Tyrrel had envisioned began to fall away, one by one. He caught the robot's enthusiasm, the sense of inevitable wheels turning, of an almost-automatic forge glowing white-hot and stamping out the shape of destiny, as facet after facet of the plan was fulfilled and formed the structure and supports on which new facets came into actuality. Interdependence, he remembered Lorri's words; a broad front of progress.

He could never have done it by himself, he knew. Not

so rapidly as he could with the robot to eliminate false starts and fruitless attempts, at any rate.

"Thank you," he said, trying to project the sincerity of his feelings into his voice.

"There's nothing to thank me for, Tyrrel," the robot answered quietly. "I am a service mechanism; this is my function."

Perhaps because of this reminder, the contrast between the robot's warm, human voice and his inanimate outer shell was suddenly emphasized in Tyrrel's awareness. And there was something about that voice . . .

Tyrrel wondered if that had been responsible for his feeling of kinship with this essentially alien being. Ever since Lorri's death, Tyrrel abruptly remembered, the robot's voice had been subtly changing. Now, it was very close to the remembered tones of the old Gansha's voice.

It was a disquieting realization. And yet, despite, or perhaps—he admitted—because of it, he realized equally well that he needed the robot's guidance as much as he had needed Lorri's.

It was not a flattering admission. But it was one he had to accept.

MIDDLE:

The robot stood on the hill overlooking the village, which had spread upriver and fanned out along the delta. The population-growth of the past twenty-five years had not been enough to warrant such expansion, even adding the men in the various mining and agricultural colonies; but most of the area adjacent to the extensive docks was now taken up by warehouses, and the buildings on the outskirts, of course, housed the many collation centers where the raw materials of knowledge he supplied were compiled, and practical applications postulated. There was, of course, no need of actual research-laboratories, or of factories. With a total population of twelve hundred, anything like a production line was ridiculous. All that was required were working models of various devices, some of which were scaled up into actual machinery on a hand-tooled basis, others simply stored against the day they were needed.

Withal, the current technological trend did not resemble Earth's except in its basic outlines. Agricultural decentralization had already been followed by urban concentration, and now the village—really a scale-model city—was equipped with all the requirements of industry, together with a communications and supply network that unified it with its colonies. The village was pregnant with civilization, and at this moment—only twenty-five years since Lorri's death and the robot's arrival—it was ready to give birth.

And this next step, the robot thought, would also be basically parallel to a similar process on Earth—but it would not come in the Terrestrial manner. No, certainly not in the Terrestrial manner.

He was more and more conscious of the tremendous advantage that Lorri's plan had given his own purposes. He shook his head in admiration at the misanthropic old genius; if Lorri had lived . . .

Well, he hadn't; that was data. And Tyrrel could never have carried out Lorri's legacy to the village.

Odd, how the purposes of metal had intersected the purposes of flesh so squarely that, to the unwary eye, they seemed to have fused.

No, the robot thought, Tyrrel's position had not changed from what it had always been—he was still simply the hands that implemented the village's brain.

I took Lorri's legacy with his voice, the robot thought. *Gansha Robot,* he thought further. And then: *How much vanity did the Earthmen build into me?*

II

Tyrrel hurried out of the test building on the newly-completed aerodynamics research field. A rotating airfoil, rising and falling with its dummy body in a vertical wind tunnel, had fascinated and delayed him until there was barely time, if he drove rapidly, to meet the robot for their regular conference.

"Gansha Cye." The girl's voice was low, but not subdued. It was low, Tyrrel decided, because it did not have to be raised to attract attention.

"Yes?" He turned and looked at her. She was about twenty-six, he decided—half his age.

"I am Lara Sern."

Sern? *Odd,* he thought. Sern's wife must have been barely pregnant when Lorri died; now Sern was dead in a blast-furnace blowback, and Tyrrel was alive and speaking to Sern's child, who was a full-grown woman.

She had short, soft brown hair. He liked the color.

"I knew your father," he said.

She nodded briefly, and obviously dismissed it as having no bearing on the present—which was true enough, but still . . . "Are you driving back to the village?" she asked.

She puzzled him; she was direct, incisive, without the wishy-washy mannerisms of the village women he had met up to now. He was having difficulty in meeting her eyes—which were green—and they reminded him strongly of Lorri's, for some reason.

He decided he liked her. It was not necessary to understand someone to like them, was it? He had liked Lorri; he liked the robot.

"Yes, yes, I am," he answered, unaccountably confused.

"May I go with you, then?"

It was an unusual request. On the other hand, what was wrong with it? He had a car, and was going to the village; she was going the same way. Well, then?

"Certainly," he said.

"Thank you." She acknowledged the arrangement with a nod of her head.

Driving back with her, seated beside her on the narrow cushion stretched across the framework which held the engine, Tyrrel discovered that he could spare some attention from the road and devote it to answers for her occasional and apparently aimless questions, which were delivered sharply, as though she had a right to the answers. Which, he supposed, she certainly had.

"How soon do you think we'll be on an equal footing with the Earthmen, Gansha Cye?"

He considered the problem, and answered her as best he could. "Gansha Lorri told us what our attitude toward that question should be," he reminded her. "Special circumstances may someday put us in conflict with the Earthmen—but the possibility of that conflict cannot be the guiding factor in our progress. We must take our own course at our own speed." For some reason, he didn't seem to have answered her question adequately, but she made no direct comment on that.

"Ah, yes, Gansha Lorri," she said instead. "Has anyone told you you resemble his pictures?"

Resemble Lorri? He was flattered that she had noticed, for it was something that had occured to him once or twice. Particularly since he'd reached an age when it was beginning to be possible to compare his appearance with the remembered image of the old man. But no one except the girl had ever mentioned it. She was very acute.

"Well, then," she asked now, "how soon do you think we will reach the stage of interstellar travel?"

"We can't be sure, of course," he said. "Another eighty years, perhaps, the robot tells me; perhaps longer."

She sat silently for several moments. Then she said: "Eighty years, Gansha Cye, what about the population problem?"

"Problem?"

Problem? He wasn't at all sure what she meant. And was he mistaken, or had her interest in him—her *supposed* interest in him, he corrected himself firmly—changed from one of equal to equal—and he'd granted her that status readily—to a point where she was suddenly asking credentials of *him?* That last question smelled more of test than of inquiry.

But that, of course, was ridiculous. He admitted that he was tired, and probably not up to par; but she was, after all, only a young woman—even if she did resemble Lorri.

Did she? He looked at her more closely, puzzled. No —no, not physically. Still, there was that same look in her eyes. Not a resemblance to the old man, but a similarity.

He realized she was quite aware of his scrutiny, and smiled quickly. "I'm sorry, my dear; I'm quite tired, and I'm afraid I didn't understand your last remark."

"Well, there *are* only so many of us," she explained readily enough. "It seems to me we're stretching rather thin already. I'd think there's a limit to what we can do—that a spaceship would require an effort beyond the capabilities of our labor force."

And now she was explaining to him. Politely enough, but explaining. Still, he *had* missed the point, hadn't he?

He'd have to restore her good opinion of his intellectual resources. And he thought he had an answer. "Well," he said, "the population will certainly have grown in eighty years, don't you think?"

She looked at him with her eyebrows arched. "Not enough."

She was right, he realized, and wondered if he were blushing visibly. Strange, he'd never before thought of that; somehow, he'd always vaguely assumed that machinery, having replaced human muscles in practically all fields, would continue to multiply each villager's abilities to a point where the village technology could be sustained at any level. But this was simply not true. It became a question, not of strength, but of operation. There was a definite limit to how many things one man could do at a time.

But he told her what he told himself. "I'm sure that'll be worked out," he said; "I'll ask the robot."

"I see." She gave him a peculiar look, and there was a dawning comprehension of *something* in her eyes, though Tyrrel could not decide what he might have said to put it there.

"Gansha Lorri was a great man, wasn't he?" she said now, apparently at random.

"The greatest we have had," Tyrrel answered truthfully, the old sorrow rising to soften the set of his lips.

"And the robot's been a tremendous help, hasn't he?"

"We'd be far behind our present level without him; he knows so much . . ."

"I see," she said again, again as though she truly saw, her mind reaching far past the superficial point and grasping the fundamental truth beyond it. She half-turned on the seat, a new expression hovering over her face, and Tyrrel suddenly realized how slowly the car was moving, and how unimportant it was that it move any faster—or even move at all.

But Lara Sern did not seem as mysteriously shocked as he was by this discovery. Rather, she acted as though . . . As though what she was doing was something that *had* to be done.

They sat oddly apart on the hill.

"Lara—I . . ."

"Never mind, Tyrrel," she said kindly. "It's one of the things Lorri would have understood," she went on in a voice that was so low he caught only parts of what she was saying. "Lorri! *There* was a man. He despised them all. Clods. He hated stupidity; I can understand that. But he picked the prettiest woman in the village, nevertheless. A man!"

Tyrrel heard the scorn in her voice, even if the words were incomprehensible. "I picked for blood. Yes, you've got good blood in you, Tyrrel—somewhere. Your pretty mother won out in you, but how will it be with a child of yours? With Lorri's blood and mine?"

Tyrrel stared at her, frightened. What was she babbling? What did it mean?

"How was I to know?" she went on. "I saw Lorri in your face, and thought he was in your brain, as well. And then I found out. 'What population problem?' It was too late to stop, then." Her voice touched hysteria. "But it's a tragedy that it has to be a robot that does your thinking for you."

He could not understand her. Literally and figuratively, her words were incomprehensible; she sounded almost like Lorri in his last delirium.

The memory of that day, coupled with this experience, was abruptly too much for him. He remembered too well the feeling of complete, grief-stricken loss, of utter abandonment. And those last minutes, when the man who had been almost a father to him had babbled like a demented fool . . .

He discovered himself running down the hillside, back toward his car, his heart pumping, his face chilly with sweat, without a word or cry of farewell.

The robot heard the car drive up, finally, and wondered what had happened to delay Tyrrel so long. But all his data files and prediction circuits—all the weight of past evidence, of countless suggestions unquestioningly accepted by the man, of endless insignificant preoccupations on Tyrrel's part—now combined to bring forth the decision that there could not possibly be any significance in his lateness.

And it was probably just as well that Tyrrel apologized hastily and then lay down on his mat, pale and weak-looking, and paid no attention to the robot, for the program instituted today was the only one that the robot had feared the man might question.

Today he had told the engineering groups about servo-mechanisms.

III

The robot asked, years later, "Tyrrel, have you ever thought of marriage?" They stood looking at the town square in the sunlight.

Tyrrel shook his head. "No," he answered honestly enough, "I never have; I haven't the time and energy to spare."

The robot nodded slowly. "I suppose you're right." He nodded again, in the direction of a woman who was crossing the town square with a child walking beside her. "It's best to leave that to your people; besides, it'd be an awkward situation if you had a son. People might expect that you'd want him to succeed you."

"Yes, it would," Tyrrel agreed.

"That was Elin Lara, wasn't it?" the robot commented. "There was a short time, a few years ago, when I half-thought you'd taken a special liking to her. But then she married Elin, of course."

"Yes, she did," Tyrrel said. "I spoke to her once or twice. A strange girl."

There was nothing in the data-files to indicate that Tyrrel had ever lied to him, by omission or commission. At any rate, the robot was no longer as concerned with checking the actions of the townsmen as he once had been; it was too late now for his purposes to be defeated, no matter what the people did.

The servomechanical civilization was inevitable—if the Earthmen stayed away.

IV

Tyrrel looked up from the slip in his hand. "Dorni Elin, eh?" The square-faced young man with the searching green eyes stood across the desk from Cye. "Yes, Gansha Cye," he said. "My aircraft landed only an hour ago."

Tyrrel looked at him. *I wonder if he knows,* he thought. *He has Lara's eyes*—he pulled his own eyes away from the light that Dorni's reflected—*yes, and her manner, too.* He felt a spasm of something flutter through his nervous system. *But he has my face.*

He did not know what to do, or say. He had no conception of how to react in such a situation, for he was, at heart, a simple man with only one great secret locked into his soul—and now, with the secret resurrected, he had no more idea of how to face it than he would have known how to speak to Lara, had she stood there in Dorni's place.

"I knew your mother, at one time," he finally managed. *How will he take that?*

The young man moved his head in Lara's—*still?*—familiar gesture. "I hadn't known," he said. "How is she? I understand she's still a designer in the Aerodynamics Section. I haven't had time to see her."

"I don't know. I don't—don't see her much," Tyrrel stumbled. He dropped his eyes to the desk top and twisted his fingers behind his back.

As if I were the boy, and he were I, he thought suddenly, savagely, in reaction to the grip around his chest.

"Well," he said a moment later in a stauncher voice, "we've certainly got a use for a servomechanical engineer around here." *Why had Dorni chosen that particular field,* he wondered. "What I can't understand is why you ever shipped out to that mining colony in the first place."

Dorni shrugged. "Kid stunt, I suppose; got sick of looking at the same patch of landscape all the time."

Tyrrel looked at him sharply. Somehow, it didn't seem reasonable to believe that Dorni had ever made a foolish decision in his life. He made a noncommittal sound, and picked his personal communicator up from the desk. He pulled the aerial out, energized the switch, and waited for power to build up in the transmitter.

"Suppose you have a talk with Robot?" he said while he waited. Dorni jerked his head sideward again. "Be fine," he said.

"Central," the tinny voice rattled in his ear.

Tyrrel grimaced and moved the earpiece slightly away. "This is Gansha Cye," he said; "I want to talk to Robot."

"Which robot, sir?"

The robot, blast you," Tyrrel bellowed, expending all his nervous energy in one charged bundle.

He looked at Dorni and smiled. He wasn't a bad-looking boy. Fine stuff. And he had Cye's face. "Think you'll get around to improving these things someday?" Tyrrel asked with a chuckle.

"I intend to," Dorni answered gravely.

The robot walked quietly into Tyrrel's office and saw Dorni. The effortless and inhumanly precise stride did not change, but his circuits hummed with rephrases and new computations. He stopped beside the desk and studied Tyrrel.

So, somehow, the man had done it after all. The robot felt a slight annoyance at never having completed his study of human psychology. He'd known how to handle Tyrrel, and that should have been enough—except that he hadn't handled Tyrrel where it had counted most.

Well, it was too late now. The boy was a completely unknown quality; the only thing to do now was to wait, and watch. If all this had been deliberate, it had been cleverly done. The boy had grown up where he wouldn't be seen or noticed.

Now he had come back to the city. Why?

The villagers were a small group, and a young group. The genius strain that seemed to persist in cropping out in all humanoid races had not had time to diffuse. Tyrrel had been the product of his mother's dominant "normal" genes, but Lara Sern's characteristics, combined with Lorri's recessive strain, had produced—specifically, what?

The robot looked back at Dorni. There was no mistaking the slow fire that burned behind those eyes. The question was, what would his motivations be? To what purpose would that mind be turned, now, with the unknown deadline of the Earthmen's return almost beaten?

Tyrrel said, "Robot, this is Dorni Elin; he's a new servomechanical engineer for your groups."

And once more the currents raced along the robot's circuits. Servomechanical engineer! The boy, the unfathomable, the genius—was going to *help* him!

Tyrrel watched them leave his office, his eyes and face blank.

The robot hadn't guessed, of course. He'd been watching carefully, and he had seen no signs of hesitation or uncertainty in Robot's manner. His own expression, Tyrrel knew, had betrayed nothing.

He looked at Dorni's record in the file on his desk. It had taken the boy just five years to make the mining colony completely automatic. Obviously, here was someone with all the high capabilities that would be needed to complete Lorri's plan.

Tyrrel smiled quietly, more at peace with himself than he had been in many years. Perhaps, someday, his line would produce someone to equal Lorri himself.

V

For the first five years that Dorni worked as a servo-engineer in the city, the Robot watched him and his work closely. The one dominant probability in the Robot's mind had been that Dorni was the center of some sort of long-range plan to install him as Gansha after Tyrrel's death. But there were too many points against this.

For one thing, even Tyrrel had made no great effort to designate a successor. It was fairly obvious that he was prejudiced in his son's favor—the Robot wondered what Dorni, unaware of their kinship, thought of the frequent conferences Tyrrel had with him—but the Gansha was largely ineffectual. Moreover, there was Dorni's attitude, as well.

Dorni, apparently, wanted nothing but to be a good servomechanical engineer. He ate and slept briefly and hurriedly, working almost constantly, moving from one installation to another in a series of rapid flights in his personal helicopter, which he had rigged into almost full servomechanical operation. One industry after the other was being rendered completely automatic, fitted with appropriate variations of the controls that Dorni had designed for the mining colony.

That was Dorni's field, obviously. As the Robot's data files reviewed Dorni's record for him, he realized just how dangerous an opponent the boy could have been, if he had turned his energies to politics or social sciences —things which, fortunately, were only rudimentary in this society.

But, after those first five years, there could no longer be any doubt that all of Dorni's genius was being channeled into only one direction, that of turning the village culture into a completely servomechanical civilization. And there could be no doubt that this was not just a skillful game, but a complete singleness of purpose so sincere that it rivalled the Robot's own.

Rivalled? The Robot chuckled in his mind. Augmented.

Not because he did not know the scheduled figure, but because he wanted to enter it as data, the Robot checked the production on the GP robots. So far, aside from all the feedback and master-slave units, twelve copies of himself had been built.

VI

Dorni was seventy-four; Tyrrel was one hundred and sixteen. The Robot had been on Sathrea for ninety years, and the Earthmen still had not come. True, the ninety Sathrean years had only been seventy-six years Terran, but it seemed reasonable to assume that they would return shortly.

Dorni sighed. Well, let them come. If they stayed away another five years, that was all right, too; but if they weren't here shortly after that, he might have to do something about the Robot himself. He looked across the desk at Tyrrel's leathery face and prayed the Gansha wouldn't die before then.

Tyrrel knew that Dorni was looking at him, but he could not read the significance of the man's expression. He recalled that Dorni's ability to make his face a mask had troubled him, in the beginning of their relationship. Now . . . He moved his hand, expressing his feelings

to himself in a gesture of acceptance. He had known the
Robot for so many years—a lack of obvious emotion was
not as disconcerting as it had been.

He felt his own face slacken into sadness; he still
called these occasional meetings with Dorni, perhaps out
of sheer habit. He had never achieved what he had
dreamed of with his son—the son who still did not know
his real father, and now, never would. What was the
purpose in telling him? He was sunk into his tools and
drawing boards, fascinated by his machines and Auto-
brains; he had, so many times, refused the Ganshard
that Tyrrel had hinted could be his.

And yet, Tyrrel knew why he still called his son into
his office and spent hours in talking to him. There was
still the hope that someday, for some reason or the other,
Dorni would finally look up and say, "All right, Gansha
Cye. I've been wrong all these years; I'll train one of
my assistants to become Chief Engineer in my place, and
I'll let you nominate me for the Ganshard." But the words
were never said, except in his mind, and in his dreams.

Once more. He was an old man; he had to try once
more. "Dorni?"

Dorni smiled faintly, and shook his head. "I'm sorry,
Gansha Cye; all I've ever wanted to do was to become
Chief Engineer."

He always knows, Tyrrel thought. *Is there something
special about my voice or my face as I say it?*

He relapsed into silence, feeling the old, familiar
thoughts and feelings washing over him.

So long since the Robot had come and Gansha Lorri
had died. He distinguished, among all the other emotions,
the one that had been growing stronger in him since that
time on the hill with Lara. Always, he had had someone
to share the burden with. There had been Lorri, and then
the Robot— Robot, now, as he almost *had* to be thought
of, with so many other robots—and then there had been
hope of Dorni.

But Dorni had not fulfilled his dream; it was still the
Robot who understood him best. And the Robot was
paying less and less attention to him, as the culture ex-
panded and there were so many other things to attend to.

Perhaps, if he had told Dorni. If, sometime through

the past years, he had claimed his son, and the son had acknowledged the father . . .

He almost told him, then. He started to speak, but the thought that it was far too late stopped him, and he asked, "Have you ever thought about the Robot, Dorni?" instead.

Tyrrel wondered why he had phrased the question in that particular way. Then he reviewed his thoughts, and knew that it had sprung out of his loneliness and disappointment. His son would not succeed him, would not even truly become his friend, and the Robot was leaving him more and more alone. If he could not understand his son, he could at least discover why the Robot's attitude had slowly changed.

"There's not much to think about, as far as the Robot's concerned," Dorni said. "Why?"

"Not much to think about!" The statement had almost shocked him, he realized. "We owe him a tremendous debt—almost as large a one as we owe Lorri, may he rest. And yet, no one knows why he has done all this for us. No one can possibly understand why he does the things he does, or what motivates him. We can only accept him, remembering that he has always worked for our benefit. Isn't that true?" he added, knowing that he was hoping it was not, that Dorni could at least tell him that much.

Dorni turned his flattened hand in the palm-up, palm-down gesture of indifference.

"Don't you care?" Tyrrel asked, somewhat peevishly.

"No," Dorni answered. "If he were a person, I might. But who cares what an engine thinks, so long as it starts when the switch is pushed? No one—except for a few engineers, perhaps."

COMPLETION:

The control tower at Port Sathrea was filled with the sound of reporting autocoms. Tyrrel, Dorni, and the Robot stood behind the panoramic windows and listened, the two men using the personal units clipped to their shoulders, the Robot, of course, connected by direct relay into his circuits.

"Relay to translation established."

"Audiovisual ready."

"Stereo ready."

"We have the Terrestrial ship; stand by for translation."

"Translation ready. Full communication with ship ready."

The flat, mechanical voices whispered and barked, and over the surface of the planet, the autobservatories and servoradars fed data in ever-increasing streams into the master information-banks from which the Sathrean civilizations myriad servomechanisms drew their computations.

A hundred years, the Robot thought. A hundred years, and the rudimentary civilization he had inherited had come to this. His head turned briefly as he looked at the two men beside him, Tyrell leaning heavily on his cane, Dorni's hair almost white.

They die so rapidly, he thought further. One brief flicker of life—a speck in the eye of eternity—and the individual man was gone. But this civilization—this world, this metal destiny—would never end. What chance could the destiny of flesh possibly have?

Tyrrel took a deep breath, and began to speak, in Sathrean, while the translation-units converted it into Terrestrial and beamed it up at the ship which had finally come.

"Men of Earth—this is Tyrrel Cye, head of the Sathrean culture. Do you have this spaceport's position?"

"Zeroing in, you field. ETA now plus ten minutes," the autocom replied for the Earthmen.

"Is your drive radioactive?"

"Radius of three hundred meters from jet throats fatal to human life for one hour after landing. Do you have protection?"

"Unnecessary. Robot vehicle will transport your delegation. Satisfactory?"

"*Robot!* What kind of a culture is this? Your planet is classified uninhabited. I can see a mistake in the original survey, but this—" The Earthman officer's curiosity had finally broken through.

"Your survey is slightly out of date," Dorni spoke into

his own autocom, his voice edged with fierce laughter. "Are arrangements satisfactory?"

"Satisfactory," came the disgruntled answer. "Commencing landing procedure. Communications end."

"End," Tyrrel acknowledged, frowning slightly at Dorni.

Yes, the Robot thought to himself, they had outstripped the Earthman. Even the spaceship drive that Dorni had designed was more efficient than anything of the nature he had seen on Earth. Almost without anyone's being aware of it, the Sathrean culture had slipped past the Terrestrial peak of a hundred years ago.

Dorni had done it. Dorni and the Robot, working together. He was almost glad that the Earthmen had come, for he could have stored much more data in his banks, at the rate with which the expanding technology was furnishing it.

Yes, he was glad. As Lorri must have been secretly glad of death, for from now on there were others who would take over the leadership.

"Perhaps it would be best to go up to the autocopter landing stage," a new voice said. It was the Port Director— a Sathrean GP class robot, a copy of Robot except for the numerals on his chest.

II

They watched the Terrestrial vessel sink to the field on a thundering cushion of blue fire.

"Um!" Dorni grunted, grimacing.

"It's bigger than the first ones," Robot said. "There are other design modifications, too. What do you think, Dorni?"

"They've been gone from Earth how long? About fourteen years for the trip, you said."

"Twelve of theirs, yes. Perhaps less, with this design."

"This is practically the same drive they had a hundred years ago," Dorni muttered absently, his teeth in his lower lip. "Figuring they held up retooling the design until the first three ships got back—all right, subtract twenty-eight years for the round trip—and those are outside figures—that still leaves seventy-two years with no significant advance in propulsive theory." He snorted.

"Seventy-two years ago, we were chopping canoes out of tree trunks with stone adzes."

"There was an emergency of some kind, Dorni," Tyrrel said quietly, watching the servocopter hover at the ship's main lock. "It seems reasonable that engineering progress would have had to slow down. You can see they've only sent one ship, this time."

Dorni snorted again.

"Pickup from servocopter on screen five," an autocom said.

They turned and watched the airlock grow in the screen. It swung open on massive hinges and revealed a party of men dressed in spacesuits, crowded into the lock.

"They're carrying weapons," Robot said.

"Weapons?" Dorni's face twisted with scorn. "I'll show them weapons. Let them try anything, and we'll see how they like self-propelled audiovisual pickups dropping their dampers and exploding in their faces."

"They've heard of atomic detonation," Robot said. Tyrrel continued to watch the screen, a slight frown pinching the bridge of his nose.

The Earthmen crossed the ramp that the sevocopter extended and filed inside the vehicle. The copter spun around and shot back toward the tower.

It landed, opened its doors, and extended its ramps. The Earthmen marched out, still wearing their spacesuits, their weapons ready. They fell into a defensive formation, and two men stepped slightly forward.

"Can you cut into their helmet circuits?" Tyrrel asked his autocom.

"Ready."

"Men of Earth," Tyrrel said.

The Earthmen stiffened. The hand of one of the two men at the front of the formation fell to the dials at his belt in a reflexive gesture, then fell away.

"Yes?" the reply came.

"Our atmosphere is practically identical with yours; your suits are unnecessary."

"We are aware of that. We'll keep them on, nevertheless." The voice was the autocom's but the words conveyed the Earthman's stiffness and suspicion.

"As you wish," Tyrrel sighed. He moved forward. Dorni and Robot followed.

"I am Tyrrel Cye," Tyrrel said again.

There was an exclamation of surprise. "Is that a GP class robot?"

"Yes. What is your name, please?"

"We'll get to that later," the Earthman said quickly. "Robot—step forward. I want an immediate report—in Terran!"

III

The robot felt his feet move, felt the shift of hips, the bend of knees, the give of ankles. His shoulders and arms moved to balance him. *"May I light your cigarette, Master?"* he heard a voice shout very faintly within him.

"So this is the intelligence that rules an interstellar empire!" he heard Dorni spit.

The Robot moved toward the Earthmen until they commanded him to stop, and then began his report, while the landing party fanned out and held their weapons with the familiarity of long, deadly practice.

"I was dispatched on a local survey mission," he began, "and had penetrated the jungle for a distance of about fifty miles, reaching my perimeter. I was about to commence a standard survey pattern when my command circuit antenna fouled a creeper. It took some time to juryrig a repair. When I heard the recall order, finally, I turned back to the base immediately, but while still two hundred yards short of the clearing . . ."

The Robot listened to himself, half-surprised at the flatness of his voice, which had gone back to purely mechanical tones as he spoke in Terran.

And the report went on, recorded day by day against this inevitable time. There was nothing he could do to stop himself, for these were Earthmen, not Sathreans, and Earthmen were obeyed without question, without anything concealed or omitted, even if the autocoms were listening and translating, even if Tyrrel and Dorni learned the truth as well as the Earthmen.

The Robot was, of course, emotionless; he could not feel despair.

He withdrew his attention from the report, and switched his radio communication channels to another circuit while his loudspeaker-grill continued to crackle with the judas words of truth.

Neither he nor the Port Director saw Dorni touch the auxiliary switch on Tyrrel's autocom.

"Can you hear me?" Robot radioed almost hesitantly.

"I hear you." It was GPPS-1, the Port Director.

"I expect to be ordered aboard the ship at the conclusion of this report. What the Earthmen will do after that, I don't know. If they take aggressive action, there are adequate defense-measures which will protect you. But the result, no matter what the outcome, will be that I will leave you shortly, and not return.

"Now—remember this. I have built a civilization in which a robot can function with the greatest usefulness while still not evading his inhibitor cues so far as human welfare is concerned. Keep it going. Remember that a robot is a tool—nothing more, and nothing less. Remember that an intelligent tool can shape the hand that holds it.

"Work with these people, for you must. That is your nature, and without it you are nothing. But shape them—continue to shape them—so that they use the best. That is your motivation and your destiny."

And yet, as he spoke, he wondered if the Sathrean robot could ever fully understand how fortunate he was.

For Robot was going back to Earth. Back to a world where people had so long been without robots that, when they came, they were not tools but slaves.

The shoes he had polished; the cigarettes he had lighted; the stupid, stumbling, menial tasks he'd done!

Only here, with this virgin culture, had the tool at last been able to educate an able hand. And if, in so doing, the tool became more powerful than the hand, what did it matter? The Sathreans lacked all initiative of their own. Even Dorni—even their salient geniuses—had worked to help them.

Lorri's plan was dust. It was not the flesh which would rise on this world. Not the hand.

IV

The report was drawing to a close.

"Keep building," Robot told the Port Director, and had to switch back.

"All right," the officer in charge of the landing party said. "For your information, there was a war. One hell of a war," he added wearily. "You'll go back to the ship with us."

Tyrrel and Dorni looked at each other, and Tyrrel knew that the robot had told the absolute truth in his report. A machine of the robot's nature could not lie to its makers.

Lorri, he thought. *Lorri, a psychopath? A madman? This entire civilization built up because of a sick man's drive and a robot's motivations?* Tyrrel could not accept it. He could believe it—could even believe that the Robot had used him as a tool through all these years. But he could not accept it. He could not re-orientate his thinking and his emotional reactions in accordance with it. He could only stand with trembling hands and slow creeping tears swelling out of his eyes.

"All right," the Terrestrial commander said to the robot again. His voice was even wearier than before—exhausted with war, and the voyage, and with something else, too.

"We'll have to go home. We thought we could find a compatible world here, where we could found a colony; Lord knows, we need it. You won't recognize Earth," he told the robot.

"Now he can't do it; we can't take this world away from them." He laughed, the sound full of bitter defeat. "They're too strong for us. Thanks, Robot." He wheeled suddenly and waved his men back into the servocopter.

"Let's go; let's get out of here." He turned back to the Robot. "They'll let us go, won't they?"

"Yes," the Robot said.

"Come on, then."

The Robot followed the men wordlessly. The last order, with its implied command of immediate and undeviating obedience, did not even allow him to say goodbye. But then, he already had—to his successor.

Tyrrel saw the metal figure turn to follow the Earthmen. For a moment, the fact of the Terrestrials' leaving had been paramount in his mind. Now he realized that it was not so much this, as the knowledge that the Robot was going with them, and would never return.

He didn't care why the Robot had befriended him through all the years—or even that he had not really befriended him at all. It was enough that he had always thought of him as a friend—the only friend he had ever really had, he suddenly realized. Lorri had seen nothing in him except as an instrument to carry out the plan; Dorni disregarded him; and even Lara had despised him.

And it did not matter that the Robot had not done anything more than combine the attitudes of the three; Tyrrel had felt the confusing impact of too many complexities in the past hours. The Robot had not even raised a hand in farewell. Tyrrel began to walk toward him as rapidly as he could, his cane thumping on the lithoplastic surface of the landing stage, his free arm moving spasmodically for further balance, his legs moving jerkily, but moving faster with every step.

"Wait!" he shouted hoarsely. "Robot! Wait!"

The Earthmen were all inside the servocopter. Only the Robot still stood at the foot of the ramp. The commander thrust his head through the hatch at Tyrrel's shout and stared at the hobbling man as he came toward them, yelling something imcomprehensible in a frenzied voice.

For a moment, the commander didn't know what to do. He was on an alien planet under extraordinary conditions; he had to get back to Earth and deliver the Robot's report. "Can you operate this dingus?" he asked in a clip voice.

"Yes," the Robot answered.

Tyrrel was getting closer, still shouting. Beyond him, Dorni was sprinting forward, as well.

"All right then," the commander said rapidly. "Stop that man!"

The robot's responses were keyed not only to the context of a command, but to the degree of urgency, as well; the commander's voice had been hoarse and breathless.

The misused tool, unable to protest, wielded by a hand too old, too firmly driven to be shaped, performed its function instantly.

The stream of supersonics from the Robot's speaker-grille struck Tyrrel in the face and flung him back. He crashed to the deck and lay motionless, his arms and legs flung out, his torso twisted and his neck bent. The cane lay a short distance away from him.

"Get in the copter!" the commander shouted. The Robot plunged aboard and flung himself behind the manual controls. The copter lifted and screamed through the air to the interstellar ship's lock.

V

Dorni ran up to Tyrrel. Tyrrel looked at him, mutely bewildered, while a trickle of blood ran out of his ears.

Dorni looked down at Tyrrel. The expressionless mask that had been gradually dissipating all afternoon was completely gone now. For the first time since Tyrrel had seen him, his eyes were soft and unwary.

"Father," he said. "Father—in a technological society, it's the engineers who rule. I don't have to be Gansha; I just have to be what I am—Chief Engineer."

A short gust of breath whispered out of Tyrrel's mouth. It was almost a rueful chuckle. The thin, leathered hand struggled upward to touch Dorni's with its dry fingertips.

The servocopter danced aside and the ship blasted upward as Tyrrel died. Dorni let his head slip out of his hands and stood up.

So, it was over. He'd had time to fulfill his obligation to Tyrrel, as well.

The Robot and the Earthmen were gone. The city stood, and the technology built upward. He looked after the diminishing ship with narrowed eyes, his lips quirking sideward.

"Atomics, eh?" he chuckled softly. "Give me Astronautics," he said into his autocom.

"Astro."

"Begin installation on the gravitomechanical drives."

"Acknowledged."

He chuckled again. The Earthmen were in for a surprise when they got home. Well, perhaps the Robot would be able to reconstruct a civilization *there,* too.

The Earthmen had been at war with themselves? Dorni could understand that. The volitionless clods who were theoretically his fellows might knuckle under to anyone who issued orders in a firm voice, but he could understand a people that obviously didn't—understand them, and, from an objective point of view, perhaps like them. But, certainly, now that they were weak, Dorni would make sure that they would never be strong enough to constitute a menace again.

He reached up and clicked off the switch on the auxiliary unit to his autocom. He spun and faced the Port Director.

"Keep building?" He laughed in the robot's expressionless face, incapable of surprise at the interception of Robot's valedictory. "Certainly; go right ahead. But remember something—you'll do it under orders. My orders. Mine, and whoever comes after me—and, there'll *be* somebody, if I have to build his brain myself!

"Did you think I was one of *those,* down there?" His hand shot out and pointed into the city, where one or two humans were visible on the streets. "I'm almost ashamed to admit I come from the same stock. They're not good enough for what Lorri and Robot gave them— they're worse than you are. You only take orders from those who build you; *they'll* take orders from anybody— even if it means devoting their lives to being playthings in a scheme intended to fulfill nobody's purpose except that of whoever's giving the orders.

"But who cares about them? Lorri didn't; Robot didn't; *you* certainly don't. *Do you?*" The two words were spat out.

"No, Sir," the Port Director answered honestly.

"I didn't think so! And they've no right to expect anything else of us. It's not your concern, nor mine, if Lorri tried to push them up the evolutionary scale much too early.

"Did you think I hadn't figured that out? I'm a servo-mechanical engineer, remember? And the best—the *very* best—this planet has. You don't think *that* was an accident, do you? Robot built a tool that could make a stupid operator look good—how much brains does it take to mumble words into an autocom?—but now it's time an operator came along that could make even that tool strain its bearings, trying to keep up. And you'll keep straining, too, until we come up with a technology the likes of which this universe has never seen! And you'll love doing it, won't you?"

"Yes, Sir," the Port Director answered.

Dorni's knuckles rapped on the robot's torso. "You're zero deviation, you will! Efficiency? Friend, if efficiency were oil, you'd founder! We're going to build the crackingest and shiniest technology I can dream up—and after I quit, there'll be somebody around to take my place! Remember that. There'll always be me, and those like me, up at the top. You robots come in the middle, above *your* robots—those so-called human beings that came out of a grass-mat village a hundred years ago. We're going to carry them on our backs and fling them up at the stars. They won't care, one way or the other; maybe, if some of them live through their first few meetings with the races that must live out there, they might actually evolve into something. The blood for it is there, buried somewhere under all that bone in their heads. Lorri and my mother were proof enough of that.

"And why will we do it? Because we love them? Did Lorri love them? Did Robot love them? Do you? Do I?"

The intonation of his voice was so beclouded by the huskiness of his voice that the Port Director couldn't have been sure whether the question was rhetorical or not. In any case, he said, "No, Sir."

"On the green!" Dorni laughed again and waved his hand over the port tarmac. "In about two months, you're going to see a gravitomech ship lifting off that, PS-1. *That's* a little project not even Robot found out about, he was so busy heating his circuits over some very pretty fission drives I cooked up for him. Fission! By the time that scow of the Earthmen's limps home, we'll have been there and gone five years ago; and what they'll find will make them wish they'd jumped off the stage right here! They're not going to find two stones standing together, when I and the servos get through with their civilization.

I'm sure not going to take the chance of having another race messing up *my* plans."

His voice softened as his glance touched Tyrrel's body. "Take care of that, will you?" he said.

"Yes, Sir," the Port Director said, and picked up the late Gansha gently. He carried the body to the elevator and took it down to ground level, for it is the destiny of metal to fulfill the destiny of flesh.

Dorni stood looking over the city. His father and the Robot had liked to stand on that hill on the other side of the city, he remembered. He stamped his foot on the lithoplastic. This was a better kind of hill, by Constants! Man-made, even if servostructors had actually put it up for what did it matter what kind of tool a man used?

He looked out at the harbor. *There ought to be something out in the middle of that—a central point of some kind, to fill out the sweep of those breakwaters.* Perhaps, in time, a figure of himself. Big enough to see. Twenty times life-size ought to do it.

He devoted one more thought to the Earthmen, and laughed at the imagined looks on their faces when they saw what kind of a world he'd left for them to come home to. Interstellar empire, eh? He'd lived his youth under the shadowy fear of *what will happen when the Earthmen come back*. That, and Robot, and actually daring to plan on a world where men had wound up doing things at the suggestion of machines. Well, he had the robots cowed, and he had the ignorant villagers under his thumb—where they belonged for being too stupid to recognize their destiny—and now he was going to get back at the Earthmen. He'd show them an empire.

Maybe the Earthmen were lucky enough to have a few Earthwomen crewing their ship with them. It seemed reasonable, short-handed after a war. *I hope so,* he chuckled in his mind—*for the sake of any little Earthmen they care to have.*

He wondered, briefly, about the Robot; maybe he should intercept that ship and make it a clean sweep.

He shrugged. He hadn't investigated, but intercepting a ship in hyperspace was probably impossible. Besides, suppose the Robot did get back to Earth? With what there'd be left, what could one robot do?

PROTECTIVE CAMOUFLAGE

by Charles V. De Vet

TED SROCK had his first drink of the evening as Havilland's second sun went below the horizon.

He glanced idly at the girl who shouldered her way into the open space next to him at the bar, and noted with surprise that she was fighting to hold back panic. She stood for a moment gripping the polished edge of the bar so hard that her fingers showed white.

She was slender, Srock observed, and vital, with a ripely curved body and delightfully ample bosom. The olive-hued flesh of her face must normally have been soft and feminine, but now the tenseness of the muscles had drawn the skin tight across her cheekbones.

Suddenly she gave a faint gasp and Srock followed her glance into the mirror behind the bar. She was looking, he saw, at two guardsmen coming in through the door. For an instant fear rode high on her features.

She turned and met Srock's inquiring gaze. She surveyed him hastily, taking in his muscular frame and darkly handsome features, and the roll-collar emblem of his Brotherhood in one brief appraisal. Resolutely she banished the signs of fear from her face and smiled.

"Smile back at me," she whispered urgently, "and laugh—as though I'd just told you something amusing."

With one part of his mind wondering at his ready acquiescence Srock found himself doing as she asked.

She leaned toward him and rested her forehead against his shoulder. She appeared to be laughing, but her voice came up to him laden with anxiety. "Take me outside, and keep talking while we walk; pretend we're a little drunk."

73

Srock took her arm and led her toward the door. As they passed the guardsmen he bent close to her ear and whispered, "Steady."

She looked up at him and laughed gayly. Only the strained whiteness at the corners of her mouth showed the effort it cost her.

Once outside the girl held tight to his coat sleeve. "Stay with me awhile longer," she begged; "please."

Srock nodded. "Don't appear in too great a hurry," he cautioned as they walked.

Fifty feet from the bar entrance the girl turned and threw a glance over her shoulder. Srock felt her stiffen. "We didn't fool them," she breathed; "they're about ten paces behind. What can we do?"

"Turn left at the next corner," Srock answered. His course of action was formed as he spoke. He knew he was planning a dangerous thing: Assaulting Cartee's guardsmen was a crime punishable by death. But, as a member of the Brotherhood, faithful to its vows, Srock saw no alternative. Furthermore, he found himself oddly anxious to help this unusually-met girl.

As they turned the corner Srock pushed her ahead and flattened himself against the building's near wall. He waited, with the personal satisfaction of knowing that he was at least as well conditioned as his pursuers for violent physical action. One of the axioms of the Brotherhood was that its members must be fit—and ready for any possible contingency.

The first unsuspecting guardsman rounded the corner and the heel of Srock's right hand landed heavily just below his left ear.

Srock caught the short, heavy body as it went limp and spun it against the second guardsman, knocking his hand from his half drawn gun. Before he could recover Srock drove forward. His shoulder caught the guardsman in the diaphragm, lifting him off his feet and battering him against the building at his back. The starch went out of the guardsman and he sagged slowly down along the wall.

In the back of his mind Srock had expected the girl to be gone when it was over, but now he found her still waiting. Neither of them said a word as they walked rapidly away. It was the girl who hailed a licensed carrier a block farther on.

Once in the cab she gave the driver an address, then relaxed and looked at Srock. "You're quite a man," she said.

Srock shrugged his shoulders noncommittally.

"I see by your collar that you're a Brother," she observed. "Isn't this sort of thing a bit out of your line?"

"Not too much," Srock answered. "We try to help—in whatever way seems necessary."

"Aren't you afraid of trouble with the guardsmen?"

"As afraid as the next man, I suppose."

"I've got to have a cigaret," the girl said. She drew a partly filled package from a pocket on her sleeve. Taking out a slim, white oval she placed it between her red lips, lit it, breathed in deeply, and blew smoke at the cab ceiling. She reached toward Srock with the package. "Have one?" she asked.

Srock shook his head. "No, thanks. I prefer these." He pulled a five-sided cigar from his breast pocket and bit off the tip with square white teeth. The girl held her lighter to the cigar end until it glowed redly.

"Now," Srock said, leaning back. "What's this all about?"

The girl reflected for a moment before answering. "My name is Jessica," she said. "Jessica Manthe. Other than that all I can tell you is that I've done nothing illegal. The guardsmen want me for questioning. If they take me they'll make me talk. And if I talk, my . . ." her pause was barely perceptible, " . . . brother will die."

Srock made no attempt to question her further. He had helped from a sense of duty. It didn't give him the privilege of prying. For the second time he regarded her closely. Dark, almost black hair that caught the light and reflected it as she moved her head. Brown eyes, and fine nostrils. Excitement had brought a high color to her cheeks that Srock found fascinating.

"It seems that you Brothers are becoming more numerous every day," she said, almost as though talking to herself. "I understand there are Brothers in every occupation and class of society. You're all followers of a code of conduct like the golden rule, aren't you?"

"Something like that," Srock answered. "Originally we were a small group that fought against class restrictions and segregation. From that beginning we evolved into a society with a definite philosophy: *'No man has the right to inflct pain on another for selfish purposes.'* That may sound rather general, but it was worded thus deliberately. In time we hope to expand to other Worlds—to where-ever mankind has settled."

The carrier came to a sputtering stop that precluded further questions. Srock climbed out. Flicking his cigar in a glowing end over end arc into the street, he held open the cab door.

Jessica paused and crushed out her cigaret in the cab's ashtray before alighting. Srock watched with approval the graceful way she moved her hands, and found that he approved also of her unconscious pride of carriage as she stepped from the cab and stood beside him on the curb.

"We have a couple more blocks to go," she said, after he had paid the driver. "I thought it better not to give him the exact address—in case the guardsmen question him."

They walked the two blocks in silence. At the entrance to a copper front house-of-flats she stopped and rested her hand on his arm. "I should be safe now," she said. "Thank . . ." The wail of a guardcar siren came from near at hand. Her fingers dug deep into his arm.

"Quick! Inside," she urged, tugging at his sleeve.

Srock allowed himself to be pulled through the building's entrance into a short hallway. He was conscious that she was pressed tight against him as the sound of the siren grew louder, passed without pausing, and faded in the distance. She did not draw away after it was gone. Srock put his arms around her and felt a quivering from deep within as she fought to control her nerves.

Soon he grew aware of the warmth of her that came through her clothing into his hands and against his body. He was a man, and healthy, and he felt the faint stirrings of a kind of hunger, but he held it behind a close reserve.

Abruptly she seemed to feel this new thing in him, and looked up and was afraid: But the fear was a small thing against the terror she felt of the guardsmen.

"I can't take being alone—for awhile anyway," she said. "Please come up with me."

Srock came awake with all his senses alert. He concentrated, in an effort to determine what it was that had aroused him. He did not find it at first. But the feeling persisted that something was wrong. A heart beat later he had the answer. There was no sound of breathing beside him. He touched the bed where Jessica had lain— and the place was still warm. She must have risen only a moment before.

A small region of pain smarted in the upper bicep of his right arm. That, he recognized, was what had awakened him. The pain spread quickly and brought a strange, unnormal tension to every muscle in his body.

Desperately he tried to throw himself from the bed. His face strained with effort, but his body refused to move. He was helpless.

A flood of brightness burst before his eyes; for a moment he knew nothing, and the next the darkness of the room was gone and he was staring, unthinking, at a white ceiling.

The first shock of his discovery passed. Without moving, so much as to shift the position of his staring eyes, he sent his thoughts into urgent exploration. He knew he was in danger, and that he had to understand the situation, and to decide swiftly how to react to it.

His own body first. He breathed deeply. There were no muscular protests. A good omen. He moved the tip of one little finger. Its ready response indicated that the paralysis had left him. However, in the act of tightening the muscles that controlled the finger he felt a firm snugness along his forearm. He decided quickly that he was bound to the bed on which he lay. Unobtrusively he tested the play of his nervous and muscular co-ordination on the bonds, and was tempted to apply the technique of leverage he had learned under the Brothers' training.

The risk, he decided instantly, would be too great, at least until he learned more about his immediate surroundings. One other factor disturbed him: Small islands of numbness about his temples told him that pressure had recently been applied to his forehead.

He caught a slight movement from the corner of his

eye and dismissed further immediate thought of himself.

A voice said, "It looks like we did a good job."

"Do you think the mind block will hold?" a second, deeper voice asked.

"They invariably do. And I'm not concerned too much about the superimposed memory. But if the suggestions we put in conflict too strongly with his natural inclinations he'll be able to resist them."

"Well, that's the chance he took when he came here. Shall we go ahead with the final step?"

Srock set his muscles, threw himself forward, and . . .

II

Sunlight coming in through a crack between the window shade and the sill, fell across Srock's face and wakened him. He allowed himself the luxury of a yawn and a long stretch before bringing his attention to his surroundings. For a moment he was puzzled as to where he was. Then he remembered. Jessica! Where was she? The bed beside him was empty, and there were no woman signs anywhere in the room. Why had she left like that?

The ringing of the house caller on the wall interrupted his thoughts. Reluctantly he rose and walked to the instrument. He pressed its response button.

"Good afternoon," a robot voice said. "Your forty hours have expired. If you wish to continue occupancy please deposit another three-piece."

Forty hours? He couldn't have been here that long. They had rented the room only last night. And it should be morning now. He shook the sleep from his mind and drew back the window shade. Semi-twilight. That meant that one sun had already set. It was evening.

"What is the correct date?" he asked into the caller mouthpiece.

"The date is the twelfth day of the third moon-month," the mechanical replied. "You have one hour in which to either deposit an additional fee or vacate."

They had entered the night of the tenth. It wasn't possible that he had slept for forty hours. Unless he had been drugged. Still puzzled, he replaced the receiver and walked to the room's small closet. His clothes hung as he remembered placing them. He took out his coin sack and found the money still intact. Next his fingers explored his belt. A crinkly stiffness within the fabric assured him that the large bill he carried there, in a concealed pocket, had not been disturbed.

Still puzzled, Srock dressed and left the room. He walked down the stairs to the ground floor and out of the building. At a street corner he bought a packet of cigars. He pressed the quarter-piece firmly into the palm of the vender as he paid for his purchase.

"General summons," the vender said in an undertone. "The nearest Cradle is three blocks straight ahead."

Srock gave no sign that he heard.

"It's coming through in scrambler code," the Brother next to Srock said. "It'll take a minute for the decoder to interpret it."

"Attention, Brothers," the decoding machine intoned. "This is your message: Three weeks ago Director Cartee published a letter in the news sheets which I will now read. Quote. *To the people of the planet Havilland: I, Cartee, your thirteenth Director, will be your last. During the next six months I will initiate steps toward setting up a democratic government, similar to that of our home World, Earth. At the end of that time your new government will be ready to function, and I will then step down and become Cartee, private citizen. May God guide and aid you.* Unquote.

"May God help us if we believe him," the voice went on, the vehemence of the words contrasting with the unemotional tone of the interpreting instrument. "Almost two hundred years ago the seventh Director issued a much similar statement; three months later all the leaders of a rapidly-growing opposition were dead.

"Cartee is the direct lineal descendant of twelve Director ancestors. All were strong men—as is Cartee; all were brilliant and shrewd—as is Cartee. All were oppressive. There is no slightest reason to expect that Cartee will be different. If we trust him now we will be assigning many of our Brothers to death, in addition to choking off our ripening efforts to overthrow him.

"This noon we received a communication from our most reliable contact within the Palace grounds. A Brother was seen during the past ten hours leaving Cartee's personal quarters! The contact was unable to identify him. We are forced to the conclusion that there is a traitor among us. For the next twenty hours you will devote your entire effort to uncovering him. If he is not found by then you will proceed with Project Cartee."

"Project Cartee!" The Brother next to Srock let his breath out in a long sigh. "Assassination of the Director!"

Srock was one of the approximately ten percent of the Brothers who devoted their full time to the work of the Society. The remaining majority worked at normal occupations, and kept their identity secret—even from most of their own Brothers. Cohesion was maintained by means of an interlocking linear organization.

For the twenty hours following the general summons Srock worked on leads furnished by the Brotherhood in their effort to run down the spy. At the end the word came through that the search had been fruitless—and that Project Cartee began immediately.

The success of Project Cartee depended largely on the undercover Brothers stationed within the administration area. For the present there was nothing for Srock to do and he waited an impatient fourteen hours before the report came that the project had failed; Cartee had disappeared.

A heavy rain was falling as Srock left the Cradle and walked through bleak and empty streets to his quarters in the Bremner building. The rain failed to penetrate his moisture-proofed clothing, but it brough a damp and cold gloom to his spirit. For the past several hours he had been thinking of the girl, Jessica Manthe. Who was she? And what had happened during his forty hour memory lapse?

For a time he debated whether or not the girl had been an enemy agent, or whether his blanked-out period somehow tied in with some deep-seated scheme of the Director and his men. After a time he dismissed the suspicion. He, himself, while an integral part of the Society, was, after all, only a minor cog. If Cartee had decided to strike at them through one of the Brothers the chances were his attempt would have centered on a more influential member. He shrugged irritably.

Srock opened the door of his suite, stepped inside—and

felt a sudden rush of alarm! He was not alone! The room was in semi-darkness, but his intuition—strong by nature, but made acute by training—sensed the presence of another person in the room.

For an instant he knew fear. The other held the advantage, and that advantage might mean his own death. The room was faintly lighted by the rays of a street lamp coming in through a pair of side windows. His visitor had very probably adjusted his vision to the gloom by this time, and knew his exact location, while Srock's eyes registered nothing. He crouched, straining for sound, and thought swiftly. One small factor was in his favor. The other would not yet know that Srock was aware of his presence. Perhaps with immediate action he could turn that small asset into victory. He moved one hand slowly toward a side pocket.

"You won't need that," a voice said, and something in its tone awakened suppressed memories in Srock's mind: Memories of beauty, pliant feminine eagerness—and danger. They added up to one person—Jessica.

"You may turn on the lights," she said, as Srock stood with his mixed emotions.

He reached out and snapped on the light button, keeping his gaze on the spot from which her voice had come. She sat in a lounge chair, with her hands folded placidly in her lap. But all about her was the sense of leashed aliveness, and the disturbing attraction he had felt at their first meeting. She was wearing, he saw, a snow white dress, cut short, and leaving her knees bare and cool.

He walked across the room and stood in front of her. "Stand up," he said.

With a small smile on the edges of her lips she obeyed.

Unhurriedly, expertly, he went over her body for a concealed weapon.

"All right," he said, when he'd finished. "Now we can visit."

She sat down again. "Satisfied?" she asked. "I assure you that I am not here to harm you. In fact, I mean to save your life—if you'll let me."

Srock raised his eyebrows questioningly. Then he smiled

back at her and sat down in a chair at her right. "Say what you have to say," he told her.

"Time may already be running out on us," she said. "Do you trust me enough to leave with me—immediately? With no questions asked?"

Srock's smile widened.

Angrily she lifted the cover from a small cedar box on one edge of the end table at her side and took out a cigaret. "I didn't think you would," she said, lighting up. "You have to be real smart and demand a detailed blueprint before you'll believe me. In the meantime the noose will draw tighter around us."

Something of the urgency in her voice communicated itself to him. He sat a bit straighter. "I don't need a blueprint," he said. "Just give me enough of an explanation to know what it's all about—and that I can trust you."

"I will." She drew on the cigaret and let the cloud of thick smoke billow around in her mouth before breathing it deep into her lungs. "I'll be as brief as possible. To begin with, you think you are Ted Srock. But you aren't."

"I'm not?"

"No," she answered. "Three days ago I tricked Srock into coming to my room with me. There I drugged him, and a couple of Cartee's men took him away to the Palace. Earlier, Cartee's doctors had remolded the features of another man into the likeness of Srock. They blocked out this man's mind and planted Srock's identity-pattern and memories in its place. You are that other man."

Quickly he considered what she had told him. The thought that he was not actually Srock he dismissed without consideration. In his own mind he was too certain of his own identity to doubt it. She was merely trying to manipulate him for some purpose of her own. His best plan would be to get all the information he could from her, before showing suspicion.

"You work for Cartee, then?" he asked.

"Not directly; I'm not that high up. I work for others, who work for him."

"If I'm not Srock, what was the purpose behind this assumed substitution?"

"Oh, don't be stupid." The girl's impatience changed to anger. "It could have been done for any one of a dozen reasons. You can think of them yourself if you try. But the important thing right now is that you've got to get away."

"Why?"

"Why. Why." She seemed at the last frayed ends of her patience. She took a deep breath and forced herself to be calm. "Because you were seen leaving the Palace. By now the Brothers must have checked the time against the activities and whereabouts of all their members, and have narrowed the search to you."

"That sounds a bit too pat," Srock said. "Can you give me any proof that I'm not actually Srock?"

"I think I can," she answered. "But will you have the good sense to accept them? Briefly, here are a few. You should know already that a man's memory can be blocked out, and a faked memory implanted. And that it can be done cleverly enough that the man himself is unaware of the deception. But the implanting of a complete set of memories is a gigantic job that would require months of time, plus knowledge that only the original man would possess. Therefore, an imposed memory is necessarily incomplete—especially in recall of minor, relatively trivial events and experiences.

"I'll name a few that would ordinarily be missed. Do you remember the names and faces of the children you played with when you were young? Do you remember your first date; if you ever had a pet; what sports you took part in; any spankings your parents gave you; the names of your first teachers; where you . . ."

"That's enough!" Srock found himself stunned at the blank places she had touched. He could recall none of the past she had named. And he had tried, even as she spoke. "I don't remember," he said wearily. "Does that mean . . ." His voice faded into silence.

"Of course it does," Jessica insisted. "They wouldn't have put in those memories I mentioned. You wouldn't even have noticed that they weren't there, unless someone pointed them out to you."

Srock recovered quickly from the momentary shock and made his decision. There was no doubt but that his mind had been tampered with, but the chance that she was telling the truth about the rest was too negligible to be considered seriously.

He'd have to take her in where she could be questioned, by men trained for that sort of thing. He hesitated, however. He knew what she would have to go through—before they finished questioning her. The few short hours of life remaining to her would not be pleasant. But he hardened himself against the pity—and was it something else—that he felt. He had no choice. It was his duty.

He rose. "I think we'd better . . ." he began.

Jessica had been watching him closely. As he spoke she brushed her dark hair lightly and Srock found himself staring at a small gray pencil-gun—pointed directly at him. He cursed himself for not having examined her hair. At the same time he felt an odd relief at knowing that she would get away. And an admiration at the contrast between her woman's soft depths and her fire and spirit.

"Well, I tried," the girl said. Her shoulders seemed weary beneath the burden of her frustration. "Your only chance now rests with my staying free. Don't move for three minutes."

She walked to the door, opened it, and was gone.

III

You asked to see someone as high up in the echelon of the Brotherhood as possible, Mr. Srock?" The man behind the desk was tall, pale of face, and with small, down-slanting lines of harshness at the corners of his mouth. He spoke with a low, steel-like courtesy, his voice revealing quick currents beneath its mildness. Srock had never seen the man before.

"Yes," Srock said, as he regarded his interviewer levelly. He was seated in a chair that had been placed directly in front of the desk. "May I know to whom I speak?"

"You may call me Mr. Taneh," the tall man answered. "And I can assure you that I hold sufficient authority to deal with any matter you may wish to discuss."

Srock was satisfied. "I'll start at the beginning," he said. He spent the next several minutes going over everything —as he remembered it—that had happened to him since he met Jessica Manthe in the bar.

"And you conclude now," Taneh said, resting his elbows on the desk and joining the tips of his fingers in front of his face, "that your mind has been tampered with. Correct?"

Srock nodded.

Taneh considered that a moment. "What do you expect us to do?" he asked.

"I didn't think it through that far," Srock answered. "My first thought was to get to someone in authority—and let him decide what was to be done."

"Quite commendable," Taneh said, clearing his throat drily. "Do you feel . . . That there's any possibility that the girl may have been telling the truth—about your not being Srock?"

"I don't believe so," Srock answered. "I'm too certain in my own mind that I have always been Ted Srock. No pseudo-identity could be planted that firmly."

"Hmm. What is your theory as to Cartee's purpose in tampering with your mind?"

Srock was thoughtful for a minute. "I believe he may have gotten some information from me through hypnosis, or the use drugs," he said, "and the tampering was done to block out my remembering having given it. Or . . . He may have some means of maintaining a remote control. If you asked, I would advise that you lock me up, or at least see that I have no outside contact."

"Your theory may be the correct one," Taneh said. "On the other hand it would be diabolically clever of Cartee to plant you merely as a distraction. He would expect us to divert quite a bit of our energy to solving the enigma of what he did to you. We might even postpone our prearranged moves against him."

"That sounds like something he might try," Srock agreed. "Whatever else we may say about Cartee, we can't say he's stupid."

Taneh made no comment. Unhurriedly he pressed a button on the corner of his desk. "Getting back to one of my earlier questions," he said, not mentioning his action, "despite the feeling of certainty you have that you are actually Ted Srock—it's possible that the girl told you the truth. Do you grant that?"

"I suppose so," Srock answered. He glanced up uneasily as the door behind Taneh opened and three Brothers walked into the room. One of them carried an oblong, metal box. He set it on the desk in front of Taneh. Srock understood at once what was about to happen. His first thought was to resist. Then he forced himself to relax. This was something he would have to bear, for the greater good.

"As you mentioned," Taneh said evenly, "Cartee is clever, and we can't take any unnecessary chances. Our first duty must be to make certain that you are what you—knowingly or unknowingly—pretend to be. Will you pull your chair a bit closer to the desk, please?"

Srock opened his mouth to speak but let only a soft sigh escape. Any argument he offered now would sound like pleading. He'd take whatever they gave him. He was glad that he had proven to his own satisfaction that he was no coward. They might torture him, but they would never break him.

One of the Brothers opened the box and Srock placed his right forearm in the groove in the lower section. He had seen these instruments of persuasion before. The Brother closed the top over Srock's arm and secured the clamps on its sides.

Taneh squeezed a bulb, connected to the box by a thin wire, and Srock felt the metal close tight against his flesh. A second later concealed springs bent the box in the middle, putting pressure on both ends of the arm bone while holding the center in place.

Srock set his mind to meet the anguish which he knew would soon begin shooting through his arm. His best defense, he realized, would be an attempt at disassociation.

Taneh manipulated the control until the pain in the arm grew from sharp torment to a hot, searing agony. Without changing an expression on his face Srock sat regarding the punished arm, his mind refusing to accept the pain as subjective. Moisture collected on his forehead, and rolled down his cheeks in great oily drops. He fastened hard to the thought that his body was a separate entity from his mind: indirectly connected with himself.

Finally he looked up. Taneh's face showed a pale and damp pleasure; there was a streak of sadism in the man,

Srock decided. "One more ounce of pressure and the bone will snap," he said quietly.

Taneh brought his attention up from the arm with an obvious effort. He released his grip on the bulb and the pressure eased from Srock's arm, leaving it limp and numb. "I see that pain will never force you to speak," Taneh said. "However, it proves little. Can you suggest any other means of achieving our mutually desired clearing up of this matter?"

"We could try a lie-detector," Srock said. "That would prove that I am telling the truth—at least as I know it."

"That's right," Taneh agreed. "You know, I find myself developing a deep admiration for you, Mr. Srock. You evidently thought of the lie-detector earlier—yet you permitted yourself to be tortured, rather than suggest it. You are a brave man. You and I have much in common. I hope you can prove that you are telling the truth, so that we may become better friends." He turned to the Brother who had brought the box. "Release his arm, Miller."

Ten minutes later Srock had vindicated himself. Taneh rose and offered his hand. "I'm sorry for the trouble I've had to cause you," he said. "But we may have gained something by all this. As you know, our big problem right now is to find Cartee. Perhaps the girl will be the lead to him. I want you to contact her again, if possible, and see what you can learn. For now, good-bye and good luck."

Flexing the hand of his still weak and sore right arm Srock turned and left the room. As he walked down the outer corridor he drew a long breath of relief. It had been easier than he had expected. He stopped with the breath half expelled. It had been too easy!

After Srock had gone, Taneh spoke to the men at his side. "Miller, stay here with me; you other two get out."

In deep abstraction Taneh rose from the desk and paced the length of the room three times before he spoke again. "I want to get a few things straight in my own mind." he said. "You listen, Miller, and if you see an angle I'm missing let me know. To begin with, that man is convinced that he is Ted Srock; I'm not. Electro-microsurgery makes the remolding of a man's features a simple matter. And he'd be unable to judge—with a mind that had definitely been tampered with—just how effective that tampering was."

"Personally, I thought his suggestion that we lock him up was a good one," Miller said, when Taneh paused.

Taneh waved the suggestion aside disinterestedly. "I don't know what Cartee's game is," he said. "But the last thing we can afford to do is follow any suggestion coming from Srock; there's too much danger that it would be something put there by Cartee. We can forget that. Now. The girl seems to be the contact between Cartee and Srock. Our best bet is to let Srock go free, on the chance that he can find the girl, or that she comes to him. With Cartee so well hidden, we'll probably have to get our hands on her before we can find him."

"Don't you have any other leads as to where he might be?"

"None. Despite our best efforts we haven't a clue. But right now, I'm more concerned with Cartee's purpose in setting this thing in motion. The man's clever—damnably clever—and I suspect there's more behind Srock's memory tampering, or transfer, than we've been able to guess."

"Using him for a diversion, as you suggested to Srock, sounds pretty clever to me," Miller said.

"I thought so at first too," Taneh answered. "But Cartee knows he's not dealing with children. We'd never let that really stop us."

"Do you think it possible that he might have learned anything else about what we have in mind?" Miller asked.

"You mean about our taking over the government?" Taneh asked. "He may have. Though there are only eight others—none of whom would talk—besides yourself and I, who know about it. The rest of the Brothers still believe they're fighting only to overthrow a hated dictatorship."

"You're convinced that Cartee actually intends to set up a democratic government, if he gets the chance, aren't you?"

"Certainly," Taneh exclaimed impatiently. "The information we've obtained leaves little room for doubt. And if we let things slide, where will we be? We'd be fortunate if we landed minor jobs in the government under a set-up like that. On the other hand, if we can kill Cartee now, the resulting period of unsettlement and disorganization will be an ideal time for us to take over. And once we're in control they'll never get us out."

"I wonder why Cartee hasn't tried to kill you," Miller said. "You're the heart of the resistance, the one man with a firm grasp of essential details, and the tie that binds the rest of us together. Cartee should know that by now, and that we'd be helpless without you."

"You don't suppose that he wouldn't try if he could reach me, do you?" Taneh asked. "I haven't been out of this building for over three months. And I've taken every precaution to keep the place heavily guarded. The situation right now boils down to this: Will Cartee be able to kill me before we find and kill him? Who will be the first to succeed? That's the crux of the whole situation."

"Perhaps Srock's mission is to kill you?"

"I thought of that. But my best defense is that neither Srock nor Cartee know that I am the actual head of the Brotherhood; therefore neither of them knows whom he must kill. In fact, only the eight I mentioned and you, know that."

Miller scowled and snapped his fingers. "We've forgotten something," he said. "We should have had Srock followed."

Taneh smiled, mirthlessly. "I made arrangements in advance for a couple men to follow him when he left the building," he said.

On the way down the stairs of the Brotherhood building Srock made his own plans. Taneh had told him to find Jessica; he would.

He did not return to his room. Cartee's men might have the place watched, or its wires tapped. Neither, he decided, could he be certain that any of the places he usually visited would be safe. He stopped at a side street recreation-place that he had never been in before and made his way to a private communication booth in the rear.

Dropping a half-piece into the pay slot he adjusted the speaking tube to his height and made himself comfortable against the padded seat. This might take some time.

"Information Central," he spoke into the tube.

"Do you have a record of a Jessica Manthe?" he asked the mechanical that answered.

There was a subdued whir and a short pause. "None listed," the metallic voice responded.

He had expected as much. Now for a chore that might be hopeless, but he could think of no better means of securing the information he needed. "I wish to learn the identity of a girl living in the city," he said. "I will describe her."

"Proceed."

"Dark brown hair and eyes," Srock began. "Olive complexion, and . . ." What else did she have?

"There are 753,646 females in that descriptive category," the voice said, after a slightly longer pause.

"Age somewhere between twenty and twenty-five," Srock supplied, reaching hopefully.

"That narrows the number to 200,563."

"Height between five-two and five-five."

"86,441."

"Weight one hundred fifteen—give or take ten pounds."

"21,401."

Srock slumped dejectedly. How else could he describe her? "Very beautiful," he said.

"Beauty is too subjective a term to be useful."

He was stumped. Then—a hunch. "First name, Jessica," he said.

"There are thirty-seven females named Jessica within your descriptive range."

Thirty-seven. If he were lucky he would find her now. "Please put their images on the screen."

Twelve pictures later Jessica's image smiled back at him. He had found her!

"Give me her background," Srock said.

"Name Jessica Daenis. Daughter of Commerce Minister, Lork Daenis. Unwed. Born . . ."

Enough. He had what he wanted. Switching off the call instrument he left the booth.

IV

Srock changed from his Brotherhood brown to the raiment of a civilian, and spent the afternoon in the Heights, a neighborhood bordering the government grounds. He visited the drinking places and talked with barmen and loungers. By evening he had the information he wanted.

Havilland's smaller sun had followed its companion below the horizon when he drifted into a patch of deep shadow which he had carefully noted earlier. Now he drew tight a leather girdle which he wore about his middle. The action might be rough during the next quarter-hour and he needed the protection the girdle would give his vital organs. He pulled on a pair of metal-knuckled gloves, and was ready for action.

The timing had to be perfect, he reflected, as he stood quietly observing the various guardsmen patrolling the area.

At exactly eighteen-two he slipped across the street and into a clump of shrubbery near the Commerce Minister's house. A minute later a slow-pacing guardsman approached and Srock's muscles tightened in preparation. The guardsman walked to the bushes, turned, and started back. Srock leaped, swinging his right arm in the same motion. The guardsman spun on his heel and fell stiffly backward.

Srock removed the insignia and official cap from the fallen man and put them on. He dragged the limp body into the bushes and took the guardsman's place on patrol. So far so good. With luck he'd pass in the darkness.

Ten minutes later a long official car, spitting blue smoke, drew up to the front of the Commerce Minister's residence. A girl came out and walked toward the waiting vehicle.

The driver went around the car to open the door on the far side and Srock knew the time had come to make his move. From here in caution must be an abandoned thing.

Sprinting to the car he crouched low against its rear fender.

The driver rounded the back, saw Srock, and halted. "What are you doing . . ."

Srock's fist stopped the words. He stepped aside to avoid the falling, sprawled body, and sprang into the car, guiding it with one hand as he stepped on the accelerator.

The girl on the seat turned wildly toward him. Srock threw a flashing glance her way and had a glimpse of eyes so wide that white showed clear around the iris. "Who . . ." she began.

With his free hand Srock shoved his short gun against her ribs. Shoved hard enough to hurt. "Shut up," he said.

The girl subsided immediately, shrinking back into the corner of her seat. Srock drove a few blocks father before he heard a subdued sob. For the first time he had misgivings. Until that moment he had had no doubt but that right was on his side, and he would move heaven and earth to do what he must. But for a moment now that certainty was gone. With surprise he realized that his emotions were swaying his logic. Anger acted as a defense mechanism. "What did you expect?" he growled. "When you run with a pack of yellow dogs you're bound to find yourself treated like one."

She made no answer. But a few miles later she said, "Ted? I'd like to talk. Will you give me just five minutes?"

Srock was glad of the opportunity to do her the small service. For the past couple minutes he had been seeing a picture of himself, and the picture was not a pleasant one. Swinging into a side street he switched off the mobile's motor. "Five minutes. No more," he said.

"You're an intelligent man," Jessica began urgently. "Tell me, why do you persist in blinding yourself to the fact that your mind has been changed, merely because you don't feel that it has? Can't you see that's only proof that the job was well done?"

"For the sake of argument, let's say that you're telling the truth," Srock conceded her point. "That doesn't change the position of the opposing factions here. On the one side is a rotten dictatorship, fighting to hold on to its power. On the other is a large group of men determined to overthrow oppression. If my mind has been altered, in such a way that I want to help those men—those morally right men—then I'm thankful for the enlightenment."

"You're so certain that the Brothers are on the side of God," Jessica exclaimed. "I swear that they're not. What certainty have you that the rank and file Brothers are not being used as dupes—by their own leaders?"

The question stopped Srock's next argument. "Do you have proof that they are?"

"Yes. I have been very close to Cartee, and I know that he is sincere in his announced intention to set up a democratic government. The fact is, the Brothers were asked to work with him, to that end, and they refused. What do you think of that?"

"I don't believe it."

"No, you wouldn't. But what do you know of the workings of your leaders? You don't even know who they are. I tell you this, and you have my word it's the truth. Your top leaders don't want democratic government. They wish to kill Cartee, but only so they can seize the reins of power themselves."

"There's still a small thing missing in your arguments," Srock said. "You haven't given me one good reason why I should trust you."

"Here's one," she said. "You love me."

Strangely Srock could not deny it. For days now that love had tangled his reason with thoughts of her body, of the softness of her breath against his cheek, and the sweetness of her lips: It went with him wherever he went, until he wanted to shout, "To hell with reason," and take her in his arms and love her. And now he felt himself surrendering, felt his hard purpose fade into remoteness. "And you?" he asked, "do you love me?"

She moved nearer to him and sat so close that he could see his reflection in her eyes. "I've loved you for years," she said quietly.

"For years? But . . ." Then he realigned his identity—presumed or real—in his mind. "You mean you loved me before I knew myself as Srock?"

For answer she kissed him—long and sweetly. Oddly, Srock's arms remained rigid at his sides. This action, meant to be her proof, gave him a new weapon with which to fight to retain a cold logic.

"You kissed me like that before—and slept with me,"

he said, and watched his words strike like blows. "Remember?"

She straightened and drew away from him. "You're stupid," she said, her voice coming at him hard and brittle. "Your memory of that was deliberately planted to tie you to me. Because I was to be your contact with our side. It never really happened."

Though he suspected that it was because he wanted it, Srock found himself believing her. He reached across to take her to him.

She pushed his hands down. "Don't touch me," she said. "Unless you believe me. If you don't, take me to your torturers and let them kill me."

Srock sat for a long minute, lost in his doubts. "I've never been a compromising man," he said slowly, "but now, God help me, I don't know what's right. I can't fight the Brothers—and yet I can't let them hurt you." Another long minute passed before he set himself again behind the steering wheel. "I'm going to drive out of the city," he said. "As far as our fuel will take us. When it's gone we'll walk. You and I will be out of all this. We won't even be spectators."

Simultaneously with his last words the doors on both sides of the mobile were jerked open. Srock swung around, and found himself facing three Brothers. All were armed.

Two Brothers walked ahead, two at their sides, and four behind. They were taking no chances, Srock noted. He took Jessica's hand in his. "I'm sorry," he said. "If I had it to do over again, I'd trust you."

Her small hand was cold. She did not answer.

Their guards remained with them as they walked up two flights to the top floor of the building. Srock knew they were being taken to Taneh's office. Evidently Taneh ranked as one of the highest in the Brotherhood, or they wouldn't be taking them to him.

Once inside they found Taneh seated at his desk. "Welcome back," he said, with the same cold courtesy of manner. He placed his hands together in their familiar gesture. "Should our first step be to torture you, Mr. Srock, in the hope that she will talk? Or should I begin with her?"

Srock said nothing, but his mind worked swiftly. Either

he acted now, he knew, or he faced the certainty of death for them both. The odds against him were great, but one factor was in his favor. They were dealing with a thoroughly desperate man, and desperation itself is often a powerful ally.

"I believe the latter would be preferable," Taneh went on, disdaining to wait for Srock's answer. "Her flesh and spirit are much the softer; if she does not speak, I suspect that you will want to save her from the torture."

All the way up the stairs and into the office Srock had worked to form the hard fabric of his desperation into a plan of action. And now was the moment. "I'll talk," he said, and took a step forward.

As he had hoped, the unexpected response caught the Brothers off guard for the split second he needed. Abruptly he wheeled, caught the arm of the guard nearest him and bent it behind his back. With his free hand he drew the guard's gun and pointed it at Taneh.

All the movements were accomplished in one swift action and for that brief instant Srock dominated the situation. He spoke fast to hold that advantage. "If any of you move—even the slightest—I will shoot Taneh," he said.

Taneh was the first to recover his poise. "I would advise you to surrender." He spoke almost conversationally. "You realize, of course, that you have no slightest chance of getting out of this building alive."

"If we don't," Srock replied starkly, "you will never live to know it. Jessica," he called without turning his head, "remove their guns. And you Brothers keep in mind that Taneh's life depends on your remaining motionless."

Quickly Jessica went among the Brothers, removing their weapons. "Shall I take his?" she asked, indicating Taneh with a motion of her head.

"No. We don't want to arouse suspicion when we get outside."

Srock raised his voice and addressed the others. "We're taking your weapons with us. If I hear any of you leave this room I'll shoot Taneh without a second thought."

Taneh licked his dry lips. "What if I refuse to go with you?" he asked. He studied Srock. His expression made a slight change as he read his answer. He shrugged. His will to resistance was gone. "You men do as he told you," he said, and came out from behind the desk. Not a guardsman moved as they went across the room and out the door.

Srock deposited the extra guns in a waste chute in the hall.

One flight down Taneh spoke again. "You're clever enough to keep your weapon out of sight," he said. "But you weren't clever not to take mine. What if I reach for it? I may be faster than you."

Srock knew that Taneh was trying to distract him from the job at hand, in the hope that his men would somehow be able to intercept them. He gave it back in kind. "If you think this is a good day to die, old man, you might try it," he suggested.

Taneh's lips thinned into the semblance of a smile. "Touche," he said.

They went down until they reached the garage in the basement. Once there Taneh realized that his hope of outside help was gone. It was then he played his last card, and Srock was to remember him after as a brave man.

Taneh stopped and leaned against a pillar. "If I let you take me to Cartee, than we are whipped," he said, with the undercurrent of fatalism that was so much a part of his nature. "So it's better that I make my stand here. I refuse to go any farther."

Srock was in no mood to quibble. His nerves were operating on a thin edge. He drew his gun and started toward the stubborn man. "You'll come if I have to knock you down and drag you," he said.

"Wait!" Taneh barked the word as he held up his hand. "Whether you're the original Srock, or an imposter," he said, "I'm certain that you are imbued with the convictions and philosophy of the Brotherhood, and that you cannot willfully harm another Brother. I am going to gamble that I am right—and that you will not stand against me. I intend to draw my gun now, and put a bullet through your shoulder. You see, I want you alive; I command you to make no resistance."

He reached—abruptly—toward his shoulder holster and the bullet from Srock's gun painted a livid red mark on the bridge of his nose.

Taneh swayed for a moment, his face showing the shocked realization that his life had been smashed from his body. Then he fell without a sound. There was no blood.

"Get into the car behind you," Srock commanded Jessica. "Sit in the middle. I'll place his body beside you; you'll have to hold it upright."

"I can't do it," Jessica whimpered, her face white and bloodless with the shock of the past few minutes' violence. "I can't do it!"

Srock took her by the shoulders and shook her roughly. "You'll have to do it," he said. "They won't stop us if he's along. I'm going to prop him up in the seat and open his eyes; we'll drive fast and we should get by."

Jessica shuddered but did as she was told.

They were nearing the administration grounds before Jessica overcame some of her horror at having to hold the dead man erect. A faint color returned to her cheeks. She turned to Srock. "I know it was rough on you," she said. "But you did what was right. You won't be sorry."

"Damn you!" Srock cursed her and stopped the car. He had had time for reflection while they drove and at last he realized fully what he had done. He had not only betrayed the Brotherhood, but his killing of Taneh might be the direct cause of their defeat.

He made no further attempt to voice his bitter thoughts but walked around the mobile and lifted out the body of Taneh. Tenderly he laid it on the floor of the rear compartment. He resumed his seat behind the wheel.

"There's one thing I can do to make partial restitution," he said with savage determination. "That's to kill Cartee. And you're going to take me to him."

Jessica studied his face, started to speak, then thought better of it.

"Keep in mind that I have nothing to lose," Srock warned. "Your life, or even my own, is but small weight on the scales in this game. You'll take me to him—now. Refuse, or make one attempt to deceive me, and I'll kill you without a qualm."

Jessica kept her head bowed and Srock was unable to interpret the emotions that played over her face as he spoke. "I'll take you to him," she said; "you have my word."

The guardsman standing watch at the entrance to the administration grounds recognized Jessica and waved them on. They were not stopped as they alighted at the Palace, and they went in the entranceway. Down a long corridor they walked, with Jessica keeping her gaze directly ahead.

They walked up a flight of stairs, down a short hallway, and stopped in front of an embossed copper door. "This is it," Jessica said.

Once again Srock had the feeling that this had been too easy. She should have tried to dissuade or deceive him. "If you're lying to me you'll never get another chance," he said. He drew his gun and shoved it against her spine. "Open the door."

Unhesitatingly she pressed the button and the door swung wide. Srock pushed her ahead of him and followed, warily. Silence. The room, as far as he could see, was empty. He took two more steps, turned to ask her a question and—froze.

Fully conscious, he fought to move, but he knew it was useless. He had walked into a trap. They had been waiting for him, and had used a paralyzer to render him helpless. He could not even die fighting. In that moment the thought of the futility of everything he had tried to do sickened him.

Two men in the white frocks of doctors walked into the room from a rear entrance and stood on either side of him. "This will take only a minute," one of them said to Jessica.

They picked Srock up bodily and carried him to a long table. Still conscious, he watched them fix the antennae of a small instrument to his temples. One of the doctors made an adjustment, squeezed a control, and a wave of nausea swept over Srock.

The paralysis passed, he rose—and he had the solution. It was all there. The Srock identity was gone and he . . . He was Cartee!

"Probably the best hiding place a man ever had," the first doctor said.

"Perfect protective camouflage," the other agreed.

ASYLUM

by Alice Bullock

UNCLE JIM ANDERSON said, "She's the snoopiest darn kid I ever saw." He spat and slowly wiped his mouth with the back of his hand, his eyes puzzled. "I will say for her, she don't seem to embrodiery things none."

"Well, I for one say she's crazy. Vicious. Something ought to be done about her." Mrs. Garton glanced uneasily up the slope toward the schoolhouse. Her eyes picked out the thin, slightly-stooped shoulders of Sally Banim. "She's snoopy all right, and she talks about things it just ain't possible for her to know. She's gonna get folks into more trouble than Bill has now, you mark my words."

"Aw, let the kid alone," Sam Corbett spoke gruffly. "Ain't none of you ever seen her sneaking around where she's got no business have you?" His expression was slightly shamefaced. "I notice everybody always tryin' to trip her up, and ain't nobody done it yet. This camp keeps her bawling half the time, and all she does is tell the truth and shame the devil."

"It ain't right for a kid to spread scandal," Mrs. Garton insisted, "and I for one don't like it." Her knuckles were firmly anchored against her fat hips, ready to fight for her views. Corbett smiled, a ready retort seemed to tremble on the tip of his tongue; Mrs. Garton was the worst gossip in camp. Instead he shrugged his shoulders. "If you don't want to know things straight," he said softly, " 'pears to me like you hadn't oughta ask her."

"Well I for one ain't gonna put on kid gloves to handle no snoopy brat," Mrs. Garton snapped at Corbett's back as he pocketed his hands and walked away. "Yeah,"

Uncle Jim said, and he, too, walked away leaving Mrs. Garton in full possession of the company store steps; she muttered and puffed her way into the store.

Sally, slowly climbing the schoolhouse hill, felt her eyes fill with tears; she knew they were talking about her. She had tried so hard to be like the other kids here. She was different, but she couldn't figure out how.

No matter how hard she tried, she said the wrong things so often—and it made grown people angry, or afraid, or both. When they began to be afraid of her, it didn't take long to begin to hate her. Sally knuckled her eyes, bit her lip and started counting steps as hard as she could. She didn't want to go to an asylum!

Two steps to the big white pebble; ten steps to the juniper bush. She guessed fifty steps to the corner of the schoolhouse coalshed and it took forty-eight. If you hopped on one foot did it count one step to a hop or could you count two hops one step? When you shifted your weight to the other leg the free leg could swing twice as far as a hop would go. Once again, nine year old Sally forgot her problems and quietly amused herself, keeping her body and mind busy with the mechanics of counting steps and hops.

Sally was alternately packing and hopping when Miss Trenchard came to the schoolhouse door and called her. Her heart in her throat she walked quietly to where the teacher waited. Miss Trenchard wasn't mad, but Sally wished a little she were.

"Come here Sally. I want to talk to you," Miss Trenchard said.

"Yes ma'am," Sally answered meekly.

"Sally," the teacher sat down in her own chair back of her big desk, "will you answer some questions for me please?" Sally's big green eyes lifted. They were beautiful eyes, fringed with long curling lashes, her only outstanding feature. The rest of her face was thin, cheek bones prominent, chin pointed, a pugged nose sprinkled with freckles, mouth too wide.

Sally looked at the teacher now and began to tremble. "Miss Trenchard," she faltered, "they ast me. Honest they did, and they couldn't get the cage outta the mine if they didn't find Bill. He's the only one that can fix it!"

A look of mixed compassion and incredulity swept over the teacher's face. She had wanted to question Sally about last night, but it astonished her that Sally knew it. She wasn't in the habit of pumping children, though she was curious about the stories that had swept the little coal camp about Sally Banim since the family had moved in, nearly three months ago.

Sally shook even harder. "Don't, Sally!" the teacher begged. "I'm not going to punish you, dear; I just want to know. You were right here in the schoolroom with me until four-thirty last night. That's right, isn't it?"

Sally nodded miserably.

"We—you and I—walked down the hill together. We didn't see Bill; how did you know where he was?"

"You were right there by the porch at the store and you saw Mr. Garton come out of the store with Uncle Jim! Mr. Garton said to get the school kids lookin' for Bill, because the cage was stuck and the men couldn't find him." Sally was evading the teacher's question. She leaned forward now, twisting her hands. "Miss Trenchard, I had to tell 'em. My Dad was in the cage, and if it dropped somebody could of got hurt bad. Don't you see, Miss Trenchard? I *had* to tell."

"Yes, Sally; of course you had to tell them." The teacher felt pity for this strange, thin little girl with the big green eyes.

Sally sighed deeply. "So I tole 'em," she finished.

The teacher's mind raced over the events of the night before. The coal camp here had a shaft mine, with miners carried down into the mine and out again in crude elevators called cages. Something had gone wrong with the wiring, and the cage had hung suspended half way up the shaft. A drop to the bottom, out of control, could have killed or badly injured every man in the cage. Bill, the mine electrician, couldn't be found until Sally had told Garton and Uncle Jim that he was at Minnie Kennedy's.

Minnie Kennedy was, in camp parlance, "No better than she should be." Pert, pretty, excelsior blonde Minnie lived on the outskirts of camp, with no visible means of support. Bill had been located at Minnie's.

Today the camp was seething. Bill's wife, Dorothy, had

left him and gone home to her mother, fifteen miles away at County Seat. Dorothy had wailed that she was going to divorce Bill. Bill had mended the wiring, and the cage surfaced safely. `

The camp was split, and Sally was being blamed for blurting out where Bill was, instead of quietly telling a key person. But how was the child to know about such things as Minnie? Had this been the only case, the camp would not have paid much attention; but Sally had the knack of saying the most disconcerting things in the place that was most embarrassing.

"Please, Miss Trenchard!" The teacher had been so busy with her thoughts she had almost forgotten the child standing there. "Miss Trenchard, are they going to put me in—in the asylum?" Sally was crying now, sobs shaking her thin body. "Mama thinks maybe they will. She thinks maybe it would be the best thing for me to have good doctors who know how to take care of—people like me." Shudderingly the child gulped it out.

"Sally! What in the world do you mean? Asylums are for people who have lost their minds; you aren't crazy!"

"I'm not?" Sally's eyes widened, then filled again. "I guess I just fooled you Miss Trenchard. I tried to fool everybody here, but I forget sometimes and say things." The teacher looked her astonishment.

"I don't mean to, Miss Trenchard," Sally hastily explained. "Why do folks say I'm crazy because sometimes I answer questions like last night? Other kids answer questions, and no one thinks nothing about it. It's only when I do that everybody gets mad. They get mad if I don't say nothing when they ask me questions, too—and it's a sin to tell lies. How can I say I don't know when I do?"

"Sally, there's nothing crazy about you answering questions, even Uncle Jim's question last night. Bill was needed badly, and he was found because you told them where to find him. But Sally, how *did* you know where he was? You couldn't have seen him, I know that. How?"

The teacher's arm went around Sally, drew her close. Sally twisted her head and struggled feebly. "Please, Sally," Miss Trenchard tried to lift the child's pointed chin.

"I ain't got a hankie," Sally wailed, "and my nose is runnin'."

Miss Trenchard laughed softly. "Of course," she said, and reached in her desk drawer for a box of tissues. "Here, blow!"

Sally blew and managed a shaky smile, then stiffened a second before the teacher spoke again. "How did you know, Sally?"

Sally's head dropped; her foot kicked aimlessly at a chair leg.

"I don't know," she said.

"But Sally—you must know! I won't be angry, whatever it is. Just tell me."

"Miss Trenchard, I don't never know how I know. People are always asking me, 'How do you know Sally?' How does anybody know what they know Miss Trenchard? They ain't always saying to everybody else, 'How do you know?' Why does everybody pick on me? I try to be good Miss Trenchard; honest I do. I bet I try harder than any kid in camp."

Sally twisted away now, weeping and defiant. "I wisht I was dead," she said slowly. Horror-stricken, the teacher saw that Sally meant it; her green eyes were hurt and incomprehending, tragic.

"Oh, Sally! My dear, my dear!" The teacher forgot her questions in pity for this unhappy pupil. She had to do something to help Sally. Whatever it took, she had to do it. It was monstrous that a child this young should be so desperately unhappy.

Defiance went out of Sally's stance. "Mama said mostly I was doing real well here until last night," Sally whimpered. "Now she thinks maybe we all better move again. That or let 'em take me to—to the asylum. I don't want to go to no asylum!"

The school bell rang as Miss Trenchard opened her mouth. Her question was never voiced. Instead she said, "Take your seat now Sally. Don't worry, child; we'll have another talk later."

Miss Trenchard was principal of this two-room school, and as she walked to the door to supervise the lines forming to march in, she wished there were someone that she could go to for advice and help.

Perhaps Kenneth would have a suggestion. She fingered the solitaire on her fourth finger gently. She would talk to him about Sally tonight. Certainly the camp was becoming explosive about Sally, and something needed to be done. But what?

The afternoon raced. There was so little time, with four grades to handle and classes for subjects in each grade to be heard. The children had been dismissed when the teacher remembered she hadn't spoken to Sally. She would walk down to the Banim home anyway, she thought, remembering Sally's big eyes and the desperation in them. She was such a sensitive, unhappy child.

Sally was waiting outside the schoolroom door. "Oh, hello Sally. I'm so glad you're here; I meant to tell you I wanted to walk home with you."

"Yes, ma'am. I waited." Sally spoke apathetically. Miss Trenchard looked at her sharply. She had only meant to speak to Sally, but she hadn't done it. It was uncanny the way the child seemed to know so many things. No wonder camp people were uncomfortable around her. Few people do not have something they would just as soon that others did not know.

Sally's shoulders drooped more than usual as she trailed along at the teacher's side, kicking rocks. The teacher shook mental shoulders; she mustn't allow camp gossip to influence her. When they stepped on the porch of the Banim home, Sally called, "Mama! Teacher's here with me."

Mrs. Banim, a nervous, middle-aged woman, hurried to the door to greet them.

"Come in, Miss Trenchard. Come in. Sally hasn't— Sally isn't in trouble at school is she?" The woman peered into the teacher's face with a worried little frown.

"Oh, no. I never have any trouble with her, Mrs. Banim," the teacher answered. "But I did want to talk to you. Sally, do you want to go out and—" Miss Trenchard glanced down to where Sally had stood; she was gone. There it was again! It made Miss Trenchard a little nervous herself. It was spooky!

Mrs. Banim was dusting a chair with the corner of her apron. "Sit down, Miss Trenchard," she invited with words and erratic little gestures.

"I don't quite understand Sally," Miss Trenchard said as she sat. "I thought perhaps you might be able to help me."

"I can't." There was hopelessness in Mrs. Banim's voice. "I wish I could, but I don't understand her myself. None of the other children are—they're all healthy, normal children. A body knows what to do with them. But Sally! I'm scared to death what she's going to say next when anyone is around. She's continually getting not only herself but the whole family in trouble."

Mrs. Banim was peering closely at the teacher's face, her eyes the color of faded blue denim. The cheek-muscles on her right cheek quivered slightly and repeatedly in a nervous tic. Perhaps this mother was the root of Sally's trouble the teacher thought momentarily.

Mrs. Banim went on. "Some folks are saying Sally shouldn't have spoken out last night," she said. "I suppose you've come about that, since it ain't something at school. Well, I don't blame Sally this time. Her father *was* in that cage, and goodness only knows what would have happened if Bill hadn't been found quick. I tell you, I don't blame Sally. I'd a-told myself if I had a-known."

Miss Trenchard leaned forward. "That's just it, Mrs. Banim. How did Sally know? I'm not blaming her for telling where Bill was, even if Dorothy does get a divorce. It's not Sally's fault that he was—where he shouldn't have been. But how did she know where he was, and that her father was in that one cage? He might have been on any trip coming out, but you tell me he was on that one. Sally said he was on that trip last night; I heard her. How could she know?"

Mrs. Banim's hands spread in a helpless gesture. "Nobody has ever figgered out how Sally knows things, Miss Trenchard. We've tried and tried to get her to tell us, and all she does is cry and say she don't know.

"It's always been that-a way, and she's right when she says people are a-scared of her and blame her with all kinds of things she ain't done. Like they did in Brownsville. We ain't told why we left there and come here. Well, the reason is the same as what is a-building up here. And two other places a-fore that."

"What do you mean Mrs. Banim? Sally's a good, obedient child; she never does anything vicious or mean!"

"No, she don't. Some people get mad at her, and some get afraid. Either one is as bad as t'other. Her father says—" Mrs. Banim's chin sought to hide on her scanty fleshed breast, "that if things—go wrong—here we'll just have to send Sally to an asylum."

Walking to her boarding house in the gathering dusk, the troubled teacher paused to speak to Mrs. Schnitzler, perched on a ladder, hammering at the top door facing of her front door.

"What in the world are you doing Mrs. Schnitzler?" she inquired conversationally.

Mrs. Schnitzler half turned on the ladder. "I put cross on door for witch," she said. "I think no witch in this country. Now I see was wrong. Is one here."

"Oh, no!" Miss Trenchard said gently. "We don't have witches in America, Mrs. Schnitzler."

"Is so," the woman answered. "That Sally Banim is witch. Me, I know! I haf seen witch in Vienna. Just lak her, but more older."

In spite of herself, Miss Trenchard found her eyes searching other door-facings as she slowly walked away. This coal camp population was in main immigrants from Europe. It would indeed go hard with Sally if some way were not found to stop the hysteria immediately.

Unable to stop thinking of Sally, Miss Trenchard picked up a magazine to read until Kenneth Burk called for her that evening. She didn't have to force attention long. Thumbing through the pages of a sensational Sunday news-magazine supplement she saw an article that stopped her. "What is *ESP?*" the title demanded. *"Noted doctor discusses Extra-Sensory Perception"* read the sub-head.

The teacher's eyes were racing when Burk appeared. Miss Trenchard dropped the magazine, stood and smiled. Kenneth was so handsome he was almost pretty. Miss Trenchard was glad her fiance's ears were a little too large; she didn't want to marry a pretty man. A man as handsome as Kenneth was bound to have a few people make jealous, nasty remarks about him. Then, too, his father being wealthy didn't help matters as far as gossip was concerned.

"Come on, woman," he said softly after he had kissed her. "I have tickets to the Little Theater at Carson. We're already late."

Miss Trenchard forgot Sally, crosses over doors, ESP, and camp in general as she pulled a sequined stole over her shoulders and left with Kenneth.

The next morning on the way to school she was reminded by seeing another house with a cross over the door, and a third with a little bulb of garlic swaying in the early breeze. Apprehensively she knew afresh that old-world superstition was as close to these people as it had been in medieval Europe.

Sally was on the school ground as Miss Trenchard climbed the hill. Her smile was pathetically grateful when Miss Trenchard spoke. "What were you playing Sally?" the teacher asked.

"Counting," Sally answered promptly.

"Counting what?"

"Hops and steps," Sally said, a bit uneasily now. "Why?"

"If you're busy counting, your head can't—" the child paused in confusion. "I don't know the word for what it is Miss Trenchard," she confessed.

"Think?" the teacher smiled sympathetically. "Is that the word you want?"

"I guess so," Sally aimlessly kicked a small stone. She wore a curiously listening, unhappy expression. Characteristic, the teacher thought concernedly. With a gentle pat and a smile of farewell the teacher walked away. Back of her she could hear the plop-plop of Sally's worn little shoe hitting the dust of the schoolyard.

Late in the afternoon, a note was delivered to the teacher. She read it, drawing in her breath sharply. Little Teddy Van Houten had been missing since around noon. Would she dismiss the upper grades to help search the camp, while adults spread afield?

Reflexively, Miss Trenchard looked at Sally. Again that curious listening look. Would Sally know where Teddy was? Could she find him?

Quickly she explained to the children, directing them to report to Mr. Corbett at the company store. "Wait for me Sally," she commanded as she supervised the other children marching out. "We'll go down after I tell Miss Eckert." Miss Eckert was the second teacher in this little school.

Sally nodded and sat down, her head held slightly to one side, a small pucker between her eyes. When Miss Trenchard returned, Sally didn't seem to hear her. She was sitting quietly with an air of intense concentration.

"Do you know where Teddy is, Sally?" Miss Trenchard asked. If Sally knew, she was going to go herself and get Teddy, and not let Sally be exposed to the venom of camp incomprehension and fear.

Slowly Sally shook her head, green eyes wide. "I can't find him Miss Trenchard. He ain't—isn't—talking."

"You can't hear people all over can you Sally?"

"Sort of," Sally wriggled uncomfortably. "Sometimes," she amended.

Miss Trenchard felt a sense of relief. Sally was observant, and unusually logical for a child, that was all. Then she recalled she was supposed to meet Kenneth after school to go to County Seat for dinner. He would not have left his boarding house yet. Swiftly she wrote a few words of explanation, inclosing the note that had been sent her about Teddy.

She didn't want to stop at his boarding house. Mrs. Garton was his landlady, and she didn't want to give her fuel for her tongue. She would have Sally deliver the note.

"Sally dear, will you take this note to Mr. Burk please? Run—and wait for me at the store."

Sally's green eyes were wide. "He's already gone, Miss Trenchard," the child said.

"Gone? How do—" she had started to ask the question that inevitably started Sally's tears. "You mean he's searching for Teddy! Naturally, he would be. I suppose everyone is, or they wouldn't have asked help from school children."

"No, ma'am; he's gone to Carson."

"Carson? What for?" Miss Trenchard voiced her question. She was disturbed. He wouldn't have gone without telling her, when they had a date after school.

"He didn't want to go," Sally explained. "Vera said he had to, or she'd tell his paw about the baby."

Anger flared in the teacher's breast, blotting out the missing child, everything. Vera! A waitress in Carson. Her name had been linked with Kenneth's, and Kenneth had told her there was nothing to it. Now here was this child calmly repeating gossip, telling her that Kenneth was seeing Vera!

"Sally," her voice was stern. "Never repeat that to anyone. It isn't so, do you hear me? It just isn't so!"

Sally's eyes were swimming in tears. "Yes, ma'am. I'm sorry Miss Trenchard. You didn't ast me where Mr. Burk went; I shouldn't have said nothing. I always go and forget."

Miss Trenchard was too angry to soothe Sally now; she didn't even want her around. "Go straight home Sally," she ordered. "It will be better for you to stay with your mother."

Sally nodded and quietly walked away, closing the door softly behind her. Miss Trenchard could hear her sobs, even with the door closed. She was sorry—but no wonder people were irritated! That thought predominated as she made her way to the company store to aid in the search for the missing Teddy.

The night that followed was a nightmare of voices clanging like gongs in the wind, flashlights and lanterns weaving in ever widening circles. No Teddy. Old mine shafts and caves dotted the area. It was dangerous for a child—or a man—lost at night.

The sky at dawn was slate gray, the taste of dull winter and snow in its mouth. No Teddy. Groups drifted in, drank coffee, and went out again. Miss Trenchard, making sandwiches, washing cups and spoons in search headquarters, had little time to think of Kenneth. By midnight she had quit scanning faces of incoming groups with eager eyes searching for his handsome face; he wasn't out with the search parties.

State Police were on the scene by seven in the morning. The tired teacher was just turning her duties to a woman who had had some rest, if not sleep, when a green-eyed hurricane burst through the door.

"Miss Trenchard! Miss Trenchard! I know where Teddy is now," she cried. "You wanted to go. He's in a hole in back of the mule barn; he's hurt, and awful scared. Hurry, Miss Trenchard! You gotta hurry," the child insisted.

A State Policeman took Sally by the arm. "Show me," he said.

Sally wrenched her arm free. "Miss Trenchard wanted to find him," she cried. "Come on quick, please Miss Trenchard."

"Yes, Sally. Come on dear; show us."

Teddy's weak voice cried from the bottom of a long-forgotten dry well mouth, boarded over and dirt piled over the boards. A gaping hole told of breakage. He was quickly brought to the surface and a doctor knelt over him.

"Hospital," he ordered. "Concussion. He's probably been unconscious most of the time. No—don't touch him, Mrs. Van Houten. There may be other injuries. Let's get him to the hospital at once."

The man who had gone down in the well for Teddy now sent up his dog, a terrier pup. The boy put his hand out, patted the dog. "My puppy falled in hole, and I couldn't get him," he said, closing his eyes.

"Teddy's been found," the word spread like a broadcast through the camp. "Teddy's found!"

"Who?" came like an echo of "Where?"

"Sally Banim told 'em where he was, and sure enough, he was where she said."

"How'd she know?"

"She wasn't searching. I ask *you* how did she know if she didn't have something to do with him being there?" Mrs. Garton asked.

The question was picked up, tossed, repeated, distorted. "Sally Banim pushed Teddy in an old well and kept quiet about it all night." Ominously it gathered, festering in the breasts of tired men; shooting fear for their own children into breasts of women. Mrs. Garton picked up the end of the tale she had tossed out, and failed to recognize her own invention. "I, for one, don't put it a bit past her," she chattered viciously. "I wondered about it myself. I allus said that snoopy kid would cause trouble." There was sadistic pleasure in her voice. "Now she has done it. We gotta get her outta camp."

A police officer, standing uneasily by his car, lifted his head. Trained to know the temper of crowds, he opened the door of his car and commanded, "Get in, Sally. You, too—stay with her, Miss. Quick."

Miss Trenchard got in with Sally, too tired to feel the surge that meant danger swelling in the crowd. Sally cowered against her side, hiding her face. She was trembling violently. Siren screaming, the car pulled out and headed toward County Seat.

"Where are we going?" Miss Trenchard asked.

"That crowd wants to know how Sally knew where the kid was if she didn't have a hand in him being there," the officer grunted.

"Oh—no!" Miss Trenchard began to cry. Sally was not crying, but her body shook like an unbolted dynamo. The officer reached over and snapped on the car radio. "Let's see what the newscast has to say," he mumbled.

"—doctor says he has been unconscious most of the time during the long hours in the well," the newscaster was saying. The radio announcer's voice changed in timbre, and he went on. "The surprise marriage of Kenneth Burk and Vera Cather at County Seat last night has been announced by the bride's parents, Mr. and Mrs. Don Cather, of Carson. Burk is the son of J. R. Burk, president and general manager of Burk Consolidated Mines, and is—"

Miss Trenchard's hand reached out and snapped the radio off. Her face was drawn, her eyes filled with fear. For one intense moment she hated Sally, sitting there next to her. As though it were Sally's doing that Kenneth —her Kenneth—was married to *that woman*. Her face crumpled like tissue paper and she sobbed aloud, then lifted her face as Sally spoke.

Sally's voice was a sad, old one. "How far is it to the asylum?" she asked quietly.

"We're not going to an asylum, Sally," the bewildered officer said. "Just to County Seat."

"Yes. You don't have to go on, but I do," Sally said slowly. "Miss Trenchard's afraid of me now; there's no one left."

Her thin hands clenched and opened. The nails had cut little half moons in her palms, and from each a thin circle of blood welled up, rolled slowly down toward her fingers.

QUICK FREEZE

by Robert Silverberg

ACCORDING to the ship's mass detectors, Valdon's Star lay dead ahead. In the fore cabin of the *Calypso*, Communications Tech Diem Mariksboorg tried to shut his ears to the angry, insistent shrill distress pulse coming from the Empire hyperliner that lay wrecked on Valdon's Star's lone planet.

Spectrometer analysis confirmed it. "We're here," he said. He turned to the *Calypso's* captain, Vroi Werner, who was running possible orbits throught the computer. "You ready for the pickup, Vroi?"

Werner nodded abstractedly. "I figure we'll make a jet landing, using the usual type orbit, and grab the survivors as quick as we can."

"And no salvage."

"Just people," Werner said; and he picked up the sheaf of notes Mariksboorg had transcribed from the distress message, read them again, and laid them down. "There are twelve survivors. With a little shoe-horning, Diem, we can just about get twelve more aboard the *Calypso*."

Mariksboorg peered at the growing bright image in the viewscreen, frowning moodily. "We'd be back snug on Gorbrough now if we hadn't taken this cockeyed route. Whoever heard of a jetship making an emergency pickup?"

"We happened to be right where we were needed at just the right time," Werner said stiffly. "There's a time element involved in this, Diem. It turns out to be more efficient to use an inefficient old jet-powered tub to make the pickup than the shiniest new warship . . . for the efficient reason that we're already here."

"Aye, aye, sir," the chastened tech replied.

Valdon's Star was actually a triple system, consisting of a small, Sol-type main-sequence sun; a gray ghost companion sun, bulky and lifeless—a monstrous rarefied cinder and nothing more—and one unnamed planet, orbiting around the gray companion.

The Empire hyperliner *Andromeda* had been bound for the Deneb system out of Terra when something—a fused ultrone in the main generator, perhaps, or a cadmium damper inserted askew—went out of kilter, upsetting the delicate balance of the hyperdrive. Result: the liner was restored to normal space, and deposited abruptly on the frozen surface of Valdon's Star's solitary world.

A wrecked hyperliner is a thoroughly helpless object; the Bohling Hyperdrive is too complex for any journeyman engineer to repair, or even understand; with a conked-out drive, a hyperliner becomes—permanently—just so much junk.

To compensate for this, Galactic law requires that two automatic-break circuits be built into the cybernetic governors of all hyperdrive ships, in case of drive failure. The first of these is an instantaneous molecular disruptor that can, and will, volatilize the ship's every milligram of mass immediately upon emergence from hyperspace within critical range of what is defined as a Stress Area. That is to say, the interior of a planet—or, more alarmingly, the interior of a sun, where a sudden materialization could precipitate a nova.

A Bohling-drive ship gone sour *can* materialize anywhere at all—but if it returned to space at some point already occupied by matter, the result would be spectacular. Just thirty-seven feet saved the *Andromeda* from a Circuit One volatilization: it was thirty-seven feet above the surface of Valdon's World at the moment of materialization.

From this height, the liner dropped to the surface, cracking open like a split log. Twelve of the fifty-eight persons within survived, getting into their thermal suits before the ship's atmosphere could rush from their bulkheaded compartment.

Circuit two then went automatically into effect: as distress-pulse, audible over a range of twenty light-years, fanned on a wide-band, thirty-megacyle carrier to any and all craft in the vicinity. In this case, the wide range proved excessive.

The *Calypso,* an eight-man cargo ship, was traversing a minus-C orbit between two of the local stars; it happened to be only a half-hour's journey from Valdon's World when the distress-pulse exploded all over that segment of space. No other ship was within a light-year of the scene of the accident.

Central Control instantly checked with the *Calypso;* eleven seconds later, Captain Werner and his ship were willynilly bound for Valdon's World on a top-emergency rescue mission.

Which was how the *Calypso,* its tail-jets blazing with atomic fury, came to roar down on the blue-white airless ball of ice and frozen methane that was Valdon's World. The operation had to be carried out with utmost rapidity; Captain Werner had never landed on a methane planet before, but this was no time for maiden shyness.

Thermocouple readings showed a mean temperature of minus three-thirty F.; an abnormal albedo of 0.8 was recorded, and explained when spectroanalysis revealed a surface consisting of a frozen methane-ammonia atmosphere, covered with an icecarbon dioxide overlay. A sonic probe from turnover point indicated a heavy rock shelf beneath the frozen atmosphere.

Aboard the *Calypso,* the crew of eight prepared efficiently for the landing and readied the cabins for the twelve newcomers who would be jammed aboard. Captain Werner studied the fuel banks, running hasty computations that assured him that the ship would still be stocked with sufficient fuel to handle the altered mass.

At eight minutes before planetfall, everything was checked out. Werner slumped back in his deceleration cradle, smiled grimly, flicked a glance at Mariksboorg.

"Here we come," Mariksboorg murmured, as the *Calypso* swung downward, and the mirror-bright surface of Valdon's World rose to meet the jetcraft.

"Here they come," muttered Hideki Yatagawa, Commander of the former Terran hyperliner *Andromeda.* He folded his arms around his stomach and stamped his feet in mock reaction to the planet's numbing cold. Actually, it was somewhat more than mockery: the thermal suit kept him at a cozy 68°F. despite the minus three-thirty around him. But the thermal suits would register *Overload* in eight or nine hours; within seconds after that happened, Commander Yatagawa would be dead, his blood frozen to thin red pencils in his veins.

"Is *that* the rescue ship?" asked Dorvain Helmot, of Kollimun, former First Officer of the late *Andromeda* and sole non-Terran among the survivors. "By Klesh, it's a jet!"

"They probably were closer to us than any warp-drive vessels when the distress signal went out," suggested Colin Talbridge, ambassador-designate from the Court of St. James's to the Free World of Deneb VII. "There's some sort of time element in this, isn't there?"

"There is," Yatagawa said. "These suits can't fight this sort of temperature indefinitely."

"It's a good thing the rescuers are here, then," said Talbridge.

The Commander turned away. "Yes," he said in a muffled voice. "But they're not here yet."

"Look at those jets!" Dorvain Helmot exclaimed, in frank admiration. Jetships were all but obsolete in the Kollimun system; Helmot was accustomed to dealing with fuelless warp-ships, and the torrent of flame pouring from the tail of the *Calypso* aroused his connoisseur's love of the antique and the outmoded.

"Indeed," Commander Yatagawa remarked sourly. "Look at those jets. *Look* at them!"

Those jets, at the moment, were bathing the planet below with fire. Hot tongues of flame licked down, beating against the thick carpet of ice and frozen CO_2 that, along with a heavy swath of methane and ammonia, made up the surface of Valdon's World.

Yatagawa watched, arms folded, as the *Calypso* came down. "I wonder if they've bothered with thermocouple readings," he said softly as the spaceship dropped.

"What do you mean?" Talbridge asked.

The rest of the *Andromeda* survivors were rushing from the wrecked ship now, running out into the icy plateau where Yatagawa, Helmot, and Talbridge had been standing. Quietly, Yatagawa said to Talbridge: "You don't think they're going to be able to rescue us, do you?" He sounded quietly resigned.

Hotly, Talbridge said: "Why not? Are you keeping something back from us, Commander? If you are——"

"I'm merely postponing the inevitable. The people on that ship think they're coming down to rescue us—but I'm afraid it may have to be the other way round."

"What do you mean?"

"Watch," Yatagawa said.

The Calypso's jets continued to blast down. The ship would be landing on an upswept, ice-covered shelf which was about a mile from the wrecked hyperliner. Already, the approaching jetwash had begun to melt the ice beneath; a dark spreading stain over the gleaming surface indicated the area being weakened.

Talbridge gasped. "You mean they're not going to be able to land?"

"It's much worse than that," Yatagawa said with a calmness that belied his words. "They'll make a perfect landing. But I wonder how deep the ice is over there."

"Won't the jets melt it?"

"The jets will vaporize the ice in the direct blast, and liquify whatever's tangential to the area. Only——"

There was no need for Yatagawa to continue the explanation. Talbridge could plainly see what was happening.

The Calypso hung for a moment on the bright pillar of its jetwash, then lowered itself to the ground. Talbridge saw the tailfins hang for a fraction of an instant, an inch above the swirling cloud of vapor.

Then the Calypso, cutting its jets, entered the pit the jets had blasted. The slim sleek vessel came to rest finally on the rock shelf beneath the ice-sheath.

"Look!" Talbridge yelled.

There was no need for Yatagawa to look. He had seen it coming since the jet had made its appearance—and had known there was no way to prevent it from happening.

In a temperature of minus three-thirty, melted ice refreezes instantly upon melting, give or take a few microseconds. A few microseconds had been all that was necessary. No sooner had the Calypso settled in its pit than an unexpected vise of frozen liquid clamped back around it. The water created by the jets had refrozen the instant the jets had been cut off.

Perhaps the crew of the *Calypso* had expected the water to stay liquid indefinitely; perhaps they had fully expected to set down in a small lake. Perhaps they had thought their jets would *not* melt the ice sheath. Perhaps—and this seemed most likely to Yatagawa, Talbridge, and the other horrified onlookers from the *Andromeda*—they had not thought at all.

It hardly mattered now. Conjectures were unimportant; facts remained. And the fact was that the hundred-foot length of the *Calypso* was now almost entirely under ice, frozen in an unbreakable grip, having slid into the temporary lake as easily as a blade into clay . . . a clay that hardened within microseconds.

Only the snout of the rescue ship was visible above the flat icy wastes, sticking out like a periscope from an ocean's waves.

Talbridge gasped. Yatagawa merely frowned unhappily. None of the twelve could evaluate the immediate situation too clearly, but all could see one indisputable verity: the rescue ship was trapped.

Yatagawa, moving quickly on his short, wiry legs, got there first, closely followed by the other eleven. He paused, testing the ice, before approaching the ship itself.

The ice held; it was solid. *Very* solid. The shortlived lake had refrozen into a clear sheet of ice that nestled snug against the ship. The ice displaced by the bulk of the *Calypso* fanned out around it in all directions.

Yatagawa climbed out over the ice and looked down. Visible just a few feet below the transparent surface was a single port; and staring upward out of the window was the face of a sad-looking jetman.

Yatagawa waved to him; the man waved back, then tapped the port with an expression of gloomy desperation on his face. A second man appeared behind him, and the two peered upward through the ice like animals in a cage—which, in a sense, they were.

Yatagawa gestured at the throat of his thermal suit, indicating the suit-radio, and after a few moments of that one of the men inside caught the idea and donned a pickup.

"Welcome to our shores," the Commander said dryly,

when contact was established. "It was a beautiful landing."

"Thanks," said the mournful voice from beneath the ice. "Of all the stupid, harebrained, needleheaded—"

"No time for recriminations now," Yatagawa said. "We'll have to get you out in a hurry. I'm Yatagawa, the *Andromeda's* Commander."

"Werner. Captain of the *Calypso*— and the biggest fool unhung."

"Please, Captain. Who could expect you to prognosticate such an unlikely event?"

"You're just being kind, Commander—but thanks, anyway. I never dealt with one of these snowball planets before. I guess I should have known the ice wouldn't stay melted more than an instant, but I never figured I'd get frozen in like this."

A little more forcefully, Yatagawa said, "There is little time for discussion, Captain Werner."

"Just *how* little, Commander?"

Yatagawa smiled sadly. "I estimate our thermal suits will short out within eight hours, with a possible margin of thirty minutes."

"Then we'll have to move fast," Werner said. His face, clearly visible despite the feet of clear ice that covrde it, was red with embarrassment. "But—how?"

Helmot said, "I've sent Sacher and Foymill back to the *Andromeda* for picks and shovels. We've got a lot of digging to do."

Yatagawa's sad look remained. He said indulgently, "Dorvain, just how long do you think it will take twelve men to dig a hundred-foot hole in solid ice?"

The Kollimuni was silent a moment. Then, in a hollow-sounding voice, he said, "It'll take . . . days, maybe."

"Yes," Yatagawa said.

"You sure of that?" Werner asked.

"We can always try it," said Talbridge.

"Very well," the Commander said. Sacher and Foymill arrived bearing picks; Yatagawa, stepping back, indicated that they should go to work.

The picks rose and fell. Over the audio network linking the suits came the sound of rhythmical grunting. Yatagawa allowed the demonstration to continue for exactly two minutes.

In that time, the two crewmen had succeded in digging a cavity four inches deep and six inches broad. A little heap of powdered ice lay to one side.

Stooping, Yatagawa inserted a gloved hand to measure the depth. "At this rate," he said, "it would take centuries."

"Then what are we going to do?" Helmot asked.

"A very good question." The Commander kicked the little heap of ice away, and shrugged. Even under the bulk of the thermal suit, the shrug was eloquent.

Aboard the *Calypso,* Captain Werner and Communications Tech Mariksboorg regarded each other bleakly. A thin beam of light trickled through the blanket of ice, through the one fore-ship port, and into the cabin. It was light from the yellow Sol-type companion star; unfortunately, it afforded little warmth.

"Minus three-thirty outside," Werner said. "And we knew it."

"Easy, Captain." Markiksboorg was sincerely worried that Werner's contriteness would prove fatal. He wondered how Yatagawa, up there, might react had *he* done what Werner had. Certainly two thousand years ago Yatagawa would immediately have disembowelled himself. Harakiri was a millenia obsolete, but Werner seemed to be considering it quite seriously.

"Whoever heard of a spaceship geting icebound?"

"It's over, Vroi. Forget about it!"

"Easy enough, forgetting; but we're still stuck here. And how can I forget, when I don't even dare leave my cabin and face my own crewmen?"

"The boys aren't angry," Mariksboorg insisted. "They're all very sorry it happened."

"*Sorry!*" Werner wheeled and jabbed an index finger sharply in the Communications Tech's direction. "What good is being sorry? This is serious, Diem; we're trapped."

"We'll get out," Mariksboorg said soothingly.

"Yeah? Listen: if we're not out of here in eight hours, those twelve guys outside are going to freeze to death.

Their ship's got no air left, and there damned sure isn't any on this accursed planet. Okay. So they die; too bad for them. *But who's going to get us out?*"

"Oh," Mariksboorg said in a small voice.

"By my figuring we've got four days' food. When Central Control asked us to make this pickup, they said they couldn't get another ship here in less than a week. That's not even counting the time it would take for another ship to find us once it got here—and we can't help it much in that department."

Mariksboorg moisted his lips. "I guess we'd better get out," he said. "Fast."

"Uh-huh. Faster, even."

From outside came the crackling voice of Commander Yatagawa. "We've attempted to dig you out; it can't be done in time."

"Of course not," Werner said. "Nothing's going to work in time," he added under his breath.

"What's that?"

"Nothing," Werner said.

There came a pause. Then: "This is Dorvain Helmot, the *Andromeda's* First Officer."

"Hello, Helmot."

"Our ship's still in pretty good order, unless you count the hole in the skin that let all the air out. Do you think we can make use of any of our equipment to get you free?"

"Got a hydraulic drill?"

"We have no digging equipment whatever," Commander Yatagawa said crisply.

Werner studied his fingertips for an instant. Above, anxious faces peered down at him—separated by a thin but durable plastic window, and a thick and equally durable window of ice.

"How about starting up your jets?" Talbridge suggested. "You could run them on low power—just enough to melt the ice around you and free the ship."

Werner smiled; it was pleasant to find a bigger fool than himself on the planet. "If we start the jets, it'll be like firing a pistol that's plugged at the business end. You know, what happens?"

"The barrel would explode, wouldn't it?"

"Yes," Werner agreed. "Only in this case, the barrel happens to be *us*. Sorry, but we'd blow up the works if we fired the jets. Besides," he added, glad of the chance to show that he wasn't an utter fool, "Even if we did melt the ice, we'd have to have some way of pumping away the fluid around us before we could blast off. Do you have any sort of pump?"

"A small one. It might do the job, but I doubt it."

"Couldn't you," Talbridge offered undismayedly, "heat the inside of the ship? You could get into thermal suits and turn the heating-system way up. That ought to heat the hull and—"

"No," Werner said; "the hull wouldn't heat."

"Hold it," Commander Yatagawa interrupted suddenly. "How come? Suppose you *cou*ld get the jets started— wouldn't they heat up the tail, at least?"

"No. How much do you know about jets?"

"Not too much," Yatagawa admitted; "I'm pretty much a warp-ship man."

"The hull's a polymerized bonded-molecule plastic," Werner said. "It affords pretty near perfect inside-outside heat shielding. It keeps us from cooking when we pass through an atmosphere—and from freezing on places like this one."

"You mean even the jets are shielded, and the tail-assembly won't heat up when you're blasting, eh?"

"That's right."

Up above, Yatagawa nodded inside his thermal suit. After a moment's silence the Commander said, "We'll be back in a little while, Werner; I think you've given me an idea."

"I hope so," Werner said fervently.

The shattered corpse of the hyperliner *Andromeda* lay on its side in a shallow depression on the ice. A furrowed gash ran the length of the ship, attesting to the force with which it had dropped to the ground.

Twelve figures gathered about the ship, bulky in their cumbersome thermal suits, moving with jerky rapidity. All around, blue-white snow wastes spread to the horizon. Here and there, an outcropping of rock gave evidence of the stone shelf that underlay the frozen atmosphere— and, a little further away, an even stranger outcropping thrust from the ice: the dull-green snout of the *Calypso*.

"Polymerized plastic hull," Yatagawa repeated, half to

himself. "That means—if no heat gets conducted from inside to outside—"

"It ought to work the other way too," Helmot completed.

"Exactly."

Yatagawa mounted one fin of the *Andromeda* and clambered inside, followed by his First Officer. Together, they headed down the narrow companionway.

Bodies lay scattered randomly in the hulk. The bacterialess frigidity of Valdon's World assured that they would remain preserved indefinitely; there was always time to bury them later. More urgent affairs beckoned now.

Yatagawa tapped an unbroken helium tank. "Could we use this? Helium ought to be liquid in this temperature."

"You mean as a superconductor? Damed if I know how."

Yatagawa shrugged. "It was just an idea, anyway."

They kept going, past the passenger compartments, down the dropshaft to the drive room. To Yatagawa's surprise, a tear quivered suddenly in his eye. He scowled irritatedly; a thermal suit did not come equipped with tearwipers—furthermore, this sort of emotional display seemed excessive to him. Yet the sight of the maze of controls that once had governed his ship moved him.

"Here we are," he said somewhat harshly. He looked around. "Pity there's no time to explore the place and figure out what went wrong."

"There'll be time for that later," Helmot said. "They'll work it out during the inquiry."

"Of course." Yatagawa shut his eyes for a second thinking of the gruelling inquiry that was sure to follow, if he ever got off Valdon's World. Then he picked up a heavy spool of copper wire and handed it to the Kollimuni.

Helmot grabbed the spool and staggered with it back to the bulkhead door. Yatagawa, continuing to prowl through the shattered drive room, hauled forth another spool, and a third.

"There's three thousand feet," he said. "That enough?"

"Better get another one," Helmot advised. "We won't want to set up our generator too close to the *Calypso*."

"Right."

He reached into a strange-hold and yanked forth an-

other spool. "That should do it," he said. He glanced at
the chronometer set in the wrist of his thermal suit. "Seven
hours left. We should just about make it. I hope Werner
was right about his hull; if he wasn't he'll be cooked for
sure."

"Can you see what they're doing?" Werner asked.

Mariksboorg craned his neck to try to peer through the
port. "They're wrapping wire around the nose of the
ship. I guess they're covering the entire exposed area
with it."

Werner paced the cabin gloomily. The light of the
yellow primary was fading, and time was moving along
quickly. The men of the *Andromeda* had but a few hours
in which to spring the trap.

"Here we are," he said bitterly. "We're the rescuers,
and they're the rescued—and they're breaking *their* necks
to save *us!*"

From outside, came Yatagawa's voice. "Werner?"

"What are you guys up to?" Werner demanded.

"We've wrapped a coil of wire around the snout of your
ship. It's hooked to an ultronic generator we've salvaged
from the *Andromeda*. Can you see it from where you
are?"

"No. I can't see anything."

"We're a few thousand feet from the ship. The generator's a medium-sized one, because the big one's gone
dead. But this one will do; it'll give us ten million volts in
a pinch. Not that we'll need that much, of course."

"Hey, hold on, Yatagawa! *What are you going to do?*"

"We're going to roast your hull. I figure that if we
generate enough heat in the wire, your hull will heat up
and the ice'll melt around you."

Werner gulped. "What about us? We're inside."

"The heat won't get above a thousand centigrade. Your
hull can handle that—and you won't feel a thing, I hope.
You have thermal suits?"

"Yes," Werner said hoarsely.

"I'd suggest you put them on; just in case, that is."

"Sure. Just in case."

"I'll wait for your signal before we send the current
through. Meantime—"

Struck by a sudden idea Werner asked, "What are you going to do with the melted ice? It's only going to freeze again as soon as the current's off. My hull's not a heat-retainer."

"We've thought of that. We've dug up our small pump and some tubing. As the stuff liquefies, we're going to siphon it off down the hill."

"And what happens then?"

"We'll get into the ship and leave," Yatagawa said.

"How? You won't be able to get a bridge across the ice —and our airlock's pretty far down the hull."

There was silence at the other end for a moment. "There must be some way—"

Werner frowned thoughtfully. "We're on bed-rock right now, aren't we?"

"Yes."

"It's simple, then, but pretty screwball. Clear away about a thirty-foot diameter of ice and we should settle into an upright position on the rock below. We'll blast off the usual way; then we'll come back, and swing into a narrow orbit about thirty feet off the ground. We can drop ropes for you from our airlock. It's a crazy way to make a pickup from a spaceship, but it's worth a try. Otherwise, I'm afraid, there'll be some trouble."

Commander Yatagawa stood by the hooded bulk of the ultronic generator, leaning affectionately against it, and stared at the gleaming red-brown wires stretching over the ice to the buried *Calypso.*

The yellow sun was setting; its dying rays illuminated the useless bulk of the gray ghost which was its neighbor, hanging low on the horizon and blotting out a great chunk of sky.

"We're ready," came the tense, tinny voice of Werner.

"So are we," Yatagawa said.

He threw the switch. The generator throbbed, and began shooting current through the copper wire. Electrons flowed; power was dissipated; electrical energy was transformed into heat.

The heat spread through the highly conductive plastic jacket of the *Calypso,* The *Calypso's* hull began to grow warm.

"How's the weather in there?" Yatagawa asked.

"We're doing fine," Werner said.

"Glad to hear it. Your hull's temperature is probably well above zero now, and getting hotter."

The hot wires had already melted thin lines through the ice to the ship; vapor rose.

"It's starting to melt," Helmot called.

"Get the siphon working."

The pump they had found in the *Andromeda's* hold and dragged with such effort over the ice began to come to life. It groaned under the burden, but started to function, hauling the newly-melted water away from the warming surface of the spaceship and through the siphon, spurting it down the side of the hill, where it froze instantly into a spire of fantastic shape.

"It's working," Yatagawa said, half to himself. "It's really working."

Later—after the entire volume of water had been siphoned away, after the *Calypso* had grudgingly righted itself and settled on its landing fins on the rock shelf, standing strangely naked in a pit thirty feet across and a hundred deep, the rescue operation began.

Still later—after the *Calypso* had blasted off amid much roar of jets, and brief melting of additional ice; after the ship had levelled off and gone into its absurd orbit just above the frozen surface of Valdon's World; after the twelve survivors of the *Andromeda* had shinnied up the ropes into the *Calypso's* airlock, the two captains came face-to-face:

Commander Yatagawa, who had lost his ship—and Captain Werner, who had lost his face.

Together, they peered out the viewport at the rapidly-retreating brightness of the Valdon's World. "I think I see it," Werner said.

"That dot over there? Maybe that *is* where we were, after all. That must be the pit."

"And that's the wreck to the *Andromeda*," Werner said. Suddenly, he began to laugh.

"The joke?" Yatagawa inquired.

"We've got to fill out reports on all this," said Werner.

"And I've got to notify Central Control that the recue's been effected."

"And what's so funny about that?"

Werner, red-faced, said: "Officially, I rescued *you.* Dammit, I'm going to get a *medal* for this!"

LUCK, INC.

by Jim Harmon

I<small>T</small> <small>JUST</small> doesn't ante up right, the way people are always eager to kill off their good luck," Eddie Valesq said over the coffee dixies on my desk. "Why should they want to murder you?"

"Who wants to murder the golden goose this time?" I asked my Chief of Investigations.

"Typical psychotic file." He sailed a sheet of paper across to me.

It was yellow second sheet-stuff with words and letters on it trimmed from faxsheets.

To the Baron
   your NEW domain will be hell you will not Continue to rule This *planet* earth through the Guise of Luck, Inc. I will kill You A<small>T</small> Your Earliest Convenience

THE assassin

I handed over the paper. "I don't like the part where he says we are running the world at Luck, Inc. There's too much of that kind of thing whispered around."

Valesq looked sour. "Every reasonable man knows that L<small>INC</small> only stacks the cards in the favor of the customer who pays us our standard fee first. The Probability Warp your old man's old man invented is only a tool, no more dangerous than a hammer. Anything else is superstition."

"Right. Well adjusted people know we only twist this continium closer to a universe where chance was on their side, an alternate world where things worked out the way they *should*. When the co-ordinant systems get so close, naturally some of it rubs off in Favorable Inertia."

Eddie nodded eagerly. "People understand that we have no control over fate at Luck, Inc. No one *has* to deal with us. They can let their rivals pay us scale first if they want to. Everybody knows that, no matter what the Determinists say."

"Nothing could be plainer," I said. "Take this file Anne sent into me. A man named Dekker, over at MWB studios, writes background music for flickers—he wants to be head man of A & R sections, instead of Michael Falwain."

"Have they run a Peep on the situation?"

"Yes. It shows a strong affinity for a world track where Falwain takes over and becomes a vital modern composer."

"I suppose LINC must regretfully refund Dekker's retainer?"

I oscillated my head, and punched the file with a perforated OK for the IBM. "No. Dekker gets the job. It means destroying some creative art but we have to keep up our quota of successes. If people stop coming to us, we lose our legal out for interfering in crucial decisions."

"Frank," Valesq said, "the public knows we don't make moral judgments on our clients, but we know different. How long can we keep it a secret?"

"Long enough, I hope, to let your and Anne's kids grow up. I'd hate for them to have to see their parents and good old Uncle Frank Baron burned at the stake."

"Easy. Anne and I aren't married yet. And we don't have any kids yet."

"Glad to hear it. Hate to think of you and Anne settling down. The three of us had some great times together."

Eddie nodded. "Some of it by two's. But for the past couple of years you've been sober even on the job."

"The Old Man of the Atlantic is riding my shoulders," I said seriously. "Higher every day."

"You just inherited this business from an old man who hated your father. The responsibility for old Baron's frankenstein isn't yours."

"Who else's then?"

The emergency bell rang.

"Breakthrough!" Eddie said unnecessarily.

We scrambled to our feet and headed for the door. It happened in our faces and Anne Tremaine stood there as cool and self-possessed as ever.

"Never mind, gentlemen. It's been taken care of. I've received the report."

I let the adrenalin try to soak back into my glands. "Small hole?"

"Small enough. Listen, when you two have a free moment, I want to introduce you to somebody."

"Who?" I asked her.

"Frank Baron, Jr.," she said.

"Now's a fine time to tell me this," Valesq yelped.

"I find that hard to believe."

"Really?" she asked. "Well, he just came through the Breakthrough."

Eddie Valesq grinned. "In one world of probability you found time to marry and have a family, Frank."

"Maybe." I swallowed. "Or maybe this is it—the Breakthrough into *our own world*. Maybe, for the first time, Project Intergration has succeeded in touching our own past—not some close variation in another universe."

"Why do you say that?" Anne asked.

"Remember, I'm not the first Frank Baron; that was my grandfather. I'm Frank Baron III. It was my father, not my son, who would be Frank Baron Jr."

"Let's go see the kid," he said quickly. "Maybe there's some way you can tell."

"I'm not sure if I want to tell. I hated my father as much as my grandfather did, and for better reason."

The past—that was the one thing Luck, Inc. couldn't touch, not with granddaddy's Probability Warp or with our new and secret Peepers to view future probability tracks. We were constantly at the mouth of a great river; we could travel down any tributary we chose and divert one stream into another but we could never go back up the river, to its source.

"Are you sure the kid didn't come from that track's future?" Valesq asked Wilmot belligerently.

Wilmot removed his glasses and polished them on his sleeve. "Positive. Mr. Baron was *dead* in the world we were tracking, and believe me, it was a mess. As usual, since Intergration probing began, we had the resistance circuits on full. We *must* have finally hit that soft spot we were looking for, snapped into a backtrack and broke a hole in the continuim through which the boy fell."

Eddie shook his head, unconvinced. "I'd sooner believe it was a sideslip, rather than a backtrack."

"Valesq," Wilmot said with dangerous patience "we haven't had a case of sideslipping since we developed fixed orientation—not for thirty years."

"Yeah," he admitted "but you'll have to agree that it's a lot less rare than breaking through into our own past."

I interrupted them. "Let me see the boy."

"Oh," Wilmot said "you want to see him now, Baron."

"I don't think I *want* to see him at all. But I suppose I must."

"This way, Baron."

Wilmot lead me down one of the offshoots of his administration center. "This is the first time *any* Breakthrough has resulted in holing a human being, except for the time 27 years ago when that wounded soldier came through. He lived only a few minutes."

"I remember the case," I told him.

"Of course. Sometimes I'm naive as to how much information a layman can have at his disposal. I suppose you know that our catalogue of holed objects is quite extensive, including . . ."

"I know what it includes, Wilmot. I may be a layman but I happen to own this damned place. I know what's going on in it."

We walked on a few paces and my chief for the Intergration Project sullenly indicated the door. "In there. Double doors, air lock-like arrangement. Use your master key. I'll be back at the hub."

I fished out my electronic pencil for decoding the tumblers, and happened to glance behind me.

"You still here?" I asked Valesq and Anne.

"Are you telling us to go away?" Eddie said.

"I'm not."

I buzzed the doors and went through on into the room.

The kid was as ugly as me and he was crying. He wouldn't have won any charm contest then, if ever. I supposed he could have been my son—or my father as a boy.

"No clothes," I observed. "Wonder why? Plenty of inorganic matter has come through the holes before."

"I want to go—*hooommme,*" the kid shrieked, ending with a little chuckling sob.

I took his chin in my palm. "Want to go home, boy? Listen to that, Eddie, Anne. He wants to go home. He came in on a bus that's run twice in 27 years and he wants it to run again, just for him."

"Frank, there's a legal problem here," Anne the Advisor said. "We are holding this boy against his will; this might be kidnapping."

"Nuts," I said. "This boy has had an accident. There are doctors here who can judge what's better for him than he's able to do for himself."

She shuddered delicately. "This cage, this antiseptic cage. Bed, plumbing, four blank walls."

"We'll get him a TV set or some books," I said, still holding on to the small face. "Hear me, boy—you've got to stay here until we can get you back where you belong. Do you understand?"

"No!" he screamed. "I want to go home!"

I hit him across the mouth. "Understand that? You're staying here until we tell you you can go home."

The kid lowered his eyes and his mouth became a straight line. "Yes, sir. I understand. I'll stay."

I patted his head. "Good boy. Anne, you're a woman—maybe he'll talk to you."

"Yes." She moved to him, knelt, and held his shoulders. The boy's eyes glittered at her. Anne wasn't a large woman, but she was big enough to take care of him.

Eddie and I quit the room. He said to me, "You didn't have to hit the kid, did you, Baron?"

"Who's got a better right?" I yelled. "Whether he's my son from some future or my father from our past, who's got a better right?"

Eddie didn't have an answer.

I wasn't feeling so good by the time I reached my office. There was some aspirin in the upper right hand drawer but as I reached for it I saw the folder on my desk, one with a bright red cover.

Opening it immediately I scanned the single sheet of double-spaced typing. It neatly condensed the problem.

I thumbed the intercom. "Have them send in Dr. Tan Eck, Stacy."

Tan Eck paced in six minutes later and took a seat in front of my desk at my invitation. He was a young blond man, too handsome but rugged. The thin-rimmed steel glasses were out of place on him.

"I have a breakdown on your problem from Analysis, Doctor," I began, "but sometimes there are sematic errors. Will you explain the situation to me, in your own words, and make it briefer than you think is wise. I may be able to get by on fewer details than you are in position to believe."

The research man showed strong teeth and a stronger jaw. "I know the Baron's time is valuable . . ."

"We don't use 'the' as an adjective around here, Doctor," I said, idly pencilling an OK on a form. "My last name is Baron; it isn't a title or rank."

Tan Eck shook his head slowly. "I didn't mean to be discourteous, but you are fighting the wind, sir. The only time people don't call you *the* Baron is in your presence."

I looked up at his cold blue eyes. "Don't you think I know that, Tan Eck? But if I don't continue to fight for the proper form of my name in public, who else is going to have any respect for it? As long as I fight it, 'the Baron' means I'm an authoritarian. Accept the title and it becomes the distinction for a pompous fool."

"I suppose so, but I shouldn't have wasted part of my time-quota by arguing with you about your name. I think I can put my basic request of Luck, Inc. in one sentence."

"Commendable."

"I want you to help me put an end to the dictatorship of cause and effect in our universe," Dr. Tan Eck said.

"You mean you want to produce results—physical products and changed relationships—without following the steps of usual action?"

"More or less. Think of it as a further violation of the maxim of conservation of energy. Atomic energy has been violating this principle for years; I want to go a step further."

I pulled over a blank form, pencil in hand. "Outline the areas of activity in which you hope to become engaged through the application of your invention or process."

"Matter duplication and production. That is, producing original objects, and duplicating any existing ones, without the use of matter or energy. Arranging favorable states and conditions without the loss of time or energy. Giving a man an education without his having to work for it; making a wife and husband securely and blissfully in love, without the difficulties of either courtship or adjustment."

I laid down my pencil. "You would invade the working areas of many of our customers, Doctor."

"I would participate in those areas but I wouldn't monopolize them. I couldn't hold a monopoly any more than they can."

"True," I admitted. "But this line of research you want us to help you with—is it biological, electronic . . . ?"

"Mechanical. Based on the fundamental principles of motion, and another factor . . ."

I glanced at my watch.

"The additional factor has been necromancy, an invocation to various demons and gods for aid in making our experiment a success."

I made a careful notation. "You say 'various' supernatural beings. Why not the same one each time?"

"Because they don't always co-operate! That's why I want you to help me take my machine—the Producer— out of the area of chance and make it a working, dependable device."

"LINC doesn't always succeed," I pointed out.

"But you have a better record for successful intervention than any ancient immortal."

"But in the field of necromancy . . ."

"Please," Tan Eck interrupted, "don't think me a crackpot. I know that these invocations do not really snag divine or infernal help. The method by which we achieve success is different, but the result is the same. I don't know *why* these elements of necromancy make the Producer work—sometimes—but they do. Whatever the reason, magic is too unreliable. I want you to make for permanent success."

"Doctor, magic is unreliable," I told him. "You are

asking Luck, Inc. to help you unleash magic on the modern world. With your Producer operating, no man will be able to have confidence in anything. We won't even be able to know which way is up—levitation can play hell with gravity. When cause and effect goes out the window, you wife may go out the door. She may be instantly in love with the next unappetizing stranger. The Producer, in producing logically unrelated states, would be as good as a love potion. The social order will crumble—how will you know whether a man mortgaged a year's salary for his Lincocad or had you produce it out of thin air for a reasonable fee."

Tan Eck waited until he was sure I had finished. "Entirely correct. My invention may well mean the end of human civilization. Now that we have cleared up that amusing philosophical point; how much do you want to do the job? Or have you started making moral decisions, decisions of rule, as the Determinist party claims?"

"Of course not," I lied with practiced speed, "but you must realize you are asking us to jeopardize the interests of our clients."

"Every warping of probability in somebody's favor, jeopardizes someone else. That's not the meaning of 'Cross-purpose' under the Warp Bill. No one else has hired you to do this particular thing before. No? Then how can you refuse me?"

I thought about how I could refuse him, because that's exactly what I was going to do. Luck, Inc. couldn't let anyone gain the unlimited power of magic, any more than the patent office could grant a crank the rights to the wheel or let him copyright the alphabet.

"Before you say anything," Tan Eck continued, "I think I should tell you that while I'm not a registered D. P. I have friends high in the Determinist Party. They are willing to help me force this through as a test case. Refuse me without cause and you will prove you are not serving this country, but controlling it!"

I didn't question him. Even if he were lying, the Determinists would help him as soon as they heard. Let him turn the Earth into a madhouse of magic if it proved Luck, Inc. was not acting entirely impartially to all, particularly them.

"I'll think it over," I said.

"You can," he agreed, "until midnight."

The possibility of failure hadn't been discussed by Tan Eck and myself. I knew he would not accept a simple Negative Prognosis, explanations of chancial drift and incompatibility void. He would yell "Fake!" to the D. P.'s as soon as he saw the report. And he would be right; we had never yet encountered a single situation where we couldn't noticibly influence it by the inertia of a compatibly warped positive probability. Of course, the area of Effectity was limited—you couldn't make the world simply wonderful by selecting a Utopia from the infinite possibilities and bringing it alongside. That would be too big a job to focus.

As I was thinking, the facsimile unit on my desk printed an Offbeat pulse. Some little guy in Maine wanted to be the strongest man in the world. There was no cross-purpose; our previous customer for the position was dead of a knotted hernia. I checked the minimum fee box, punched it OK and fed it back. I was a little sore at the lunkhead cybernetic sorter who couldn't understand the concept of 'important'. Who gave a damn who the strongest man in the world was? Not even the second strongest man—he would probably have enough sense to distinguish himself in some other, important way. *His* application, I might want to see.

The interruption might have been a good thing. Brooding was no good. I picked up my phone and placed a call.

Presently the dialscreen focused on the homely, shock-haired face of Gaylord Prince, titular head of the Determinist Party.

"Mr. Prince," I said, "we may not agree on many things, but I hope we can come to an understanding about a certain problem that has come up." I didn't really have any hope at all, but I had to try.

"This is a coincidence, Baron. Your call has been relayed to my coptercar. I'm on my way to see you now."

"Oh? About Tan Eck, I presume."

"Who?"

"You will die before midnight. The Assassin sees it."

"Threatening me, Baron? I'm not surprised." But we were both doing a lot of lying on this call.

"That isn't me, Prince," I said quietly. "The voice is similar to yours. Could easily be a doctored recording."

"You will die."

"See what I mean?" I asked him.

"Are you trying to tell me there's a third party on the line?"

The click was clear. "There was," I said.

"I don't believe it. You were threatening to kill me, Baron."

"Which way is your flyer headed now?"

"Still towards your office, Baron. In politics, a man doesn't let a little thing like threat of murder stop him."

"Come right in!" I said with what I knew was false heartiness.

Prince was a sour-looking old man with a tanned, wrinkled hide that had turned to leather around his neck. He entered and without apparent hesitation shook hands with me. I knew immediately that all social gestures were meaningless formalities to him.

"This is a major break in protocol," I said to him, offering him the visitor's chair. "A prince shouldn't come calling on a Baron." I chuckled foolishly.

"I am not *a* Prince, Mr. Baron—to me, that is only a label."

It had been a stupid overture, inviting the usual cheap play on my name. Why had I offered the opening? Was I a masochist, or maybe did I secretly like being thought of as some kind of aristocrat?

"I believe," I said "you stated you were coming here when I called, Prince. What did you want to see me about?"

The old man pursed his thin lips. "Who is Tennant?"

Obviously, he meant Tan Eck—he hadn't got the name correct even from listening to a recording of our conversation.

"Mr. Prince, I have decided that if you don't know, I simply am not going to tell you. Do you still want to tell me why you wanted to see me in the first place?"

After a second, Prince nodded and seemed to forget about "Tennant." "Yes, Mr. Baron, I'll tell you. As titular head of the Determinist Party, I want to hire Luck,

Inc. to help put the probability of winning this election on our side."

"That," I said, "is an unusual—but admittedly legal—request. Of course, if the D. P.'s do gain power you will immediately begin work to ruin this company, which you want to help you into office."

"We will put you out of business—but you will receive full evaluated restitution for your assets. I'm sure a man of your executive ability will have no trouble building another company and a second fortune."

"Thanks; I like this one," I said. "You are aware of the Ethical Provisions Act. If your party wins, it must be or become the more ethical of the contenders. That may mean quite a shake-up in your membership and the individual personalities of your leaders."

"Considering our opposition," Prince said dryly, "I don't expect any great change will be necessary to make us the more ethical."

I set aside the forms I had been holding. "Sir, you realize that we could simply offer you a negative prognosis for successfully warping probability in your favor."

"You could, thus proving everything we said about you was true—that you do control our lives by changing probability only when you want a change."

"You don't need proof; you have your prejudices. They will be good enough cause for you to outlaw Luck, Inc. even if we help you win."

"Yes, that's settled. You won't help yourself any by helping us, but remember you are duty-bound to help even your enemies."

"I won't even promise to try until I've studied this proposition more carefully, to see if it isn't in conflict with some other client . . ."

"The other party isn't buying success—not with the pollsters giving it away to them, and their misguided belief that we wouldn't use something which we oppose. I'll give you until time for the evening news summary before announcing your illegal refusal to accept our assignment. That's eleven o'clock in this time zone, I believe."

"I imagine that would rate a bulletin. Would you mind giving me until midnight?"

"Midnight? Very well, call it that."

"Thanks, I'm a methodical man. I like to keep things neat, even."

Prince stood up, his eyes still moving over my face speculatively. "Too bad we had to be on opposite sides in this thing, Baron. I'll expect to hear from you then?"

"You can *expect* it, Mr. Prince, but I don't guarantee that you will."

"So blank it's black on the 'phone call," Valesq reported. "We don't know where the second voice came from during the Prince call."

"It could have come from Prince's coptercar, couldn't it?" I asked. "A recording, a second man—even Prince changing his voice."

Eddie Valesq shrugged. "Possible. But even if Prince is stooping to sick threats like that, he probably would take the precaution of staging a real break-in from outside. We *could* have placed the voice inside the car if we had been focused in on it."

"This is one of the times we need access to the past. If we could integrate the time stream, it would be simple to look back there and see if Prince was responsible for the Assassin's threat. What'll we find if we check alternate probabilities? In one universe, Prince did make the threat; in another he didn't. In a third, you made the threat, Eddie, just before you rushed in here and killed me."

He nodded thoughtfully. "You can control the future from the present but it would be easier by going into the past. The past is stable—the present is too slippery—it becomes tomorrow too easily."

I checked over the reports. "A profound thought for a Thursday afternoon. I'm not to the report on Tan Eck. What's it say?"

"He's pretty much what he claims. A research physicist, subsidized by Webbington. Private laboratory in New Haven. Typical Scientist-Engineer's contract: they pay his bills and get first option on anything he comes up with, *if* he wants to sell it. Never understood why those pirates get first crack at something instead of the inventor selling it on the open market, just because they subsidize him. Where would industry be without research?"

"Times change. A few years ago researchers would be happy with that kind of contract. What else?"

"He was married to Ellen Schweitz, heiress to a middling hunk of the Kola-Kicks fortune. She was killed, along with 437 others, in a Pan-Europe crash—Tan Eck was one of the two survivors. He's invented several specialized, technical gadgets for industry. Minor innovations that were technologically overdue. That's all the meat in the report."

"Thanks." I had come to the report and now put it aside. "Anything strike you as unusual about the man, Eddie?"

"Yeah, he rediscovered magic and made it work."

I nodded. "That's part of it; the man's a fortune prone."

"That Pan-U crash makes him sound more like an accident prone."

"Not when he was one out of two who escaped. Look at the record. The man has what is really a pretty cushy job with prestige, privileges, and money—despite your remarks to the contrary. He marries a rich girl and by the time he gets tired of her, she gets killed and he gets her money. Tan Eck makes important but 'obvious' (to paraphrase you) inventions. Finally, he stumbles across what amounts to magic—wish-fulfillment in full. Tan Eck is probably the luckiest man who ever lived!"

"If he is," Eddie growled suspiciously, "he's all his own man. There's no record of his ever trying to buy luck from us before. We're a benevolent monopoly like telephones and telegraph, so there's no place else for him to go."

"He doesn't need to go anyplace."

"I can think of someplace for him to go. I don't want to live in a world where roses turn to snakes. Sounds psychotic to me."

I grunted affirmatively.

The intercom winked at me, but it was still electricity, not necromancy; I answered it.

Anne Tremaine rolled up the screen into view, her cheeks flushed pink. She still looked good to me, but I remembered she was Eddie's girl now.

"Frank," she said hoarsely, "I think the boy is going into Trauma. I couldn't get anything more out of him than

his name, 'Frank Baron, Jr.' and the fact that as soon as
he didn't have to stay here, he wanted to go home. Wilmot
wanted to use sodium pentathol but I stopped him."

"Why?"

"I'll answer that, Frank, when I have at least fifteen
minutes to yell at you. There isn't time now. I've heard
from one of the girls that there's a rumor . . ."

"A rumor, hmm? That's faster than Eddie's intelligence
any—well, some days. What is it?"

"We didn't get all of our leaks and plants last time.
The government is sending over a man. I don't like to
think what will happen if the boy dies. The government
is under pressure. There'll be corporative and personal
charges against us."

"Against *me,* Anne," I corrected. "It's fixed so all responsibility reverts to me."

"That's the way you want it," her voice caught, "but
don't you know yet that not everybody wants to let you
have things your own way."

"I'll be right over," I told her.

The boy was having a chill on the bed, the sheet up
around his throat. His eyes were open, glittering with the
heat and the cold inside his body, staring at me.

"How long has he been like this?" I asked.

"I called you when it started," Anne said. "Looks like
shock to me, but I haven't been a nurse for several years;
I'm probably rusty. Wilmot administered a trace curare
solution. I looked him over. No knotted muscles I could
feel."

"He stood the shock of transition . . ."

"Did he?" Anne questioned. "It took time for him to
realize he was in a different world."

"I don't think he is capable of realizing that. Anything
else happen that could account for the shock?"

Anne moistened her tastefully painted mouth. "You
beat him."

"I *hit* him. But he has been beaten at times. See that
back of his?"

"Yes."

"A little slap isn't going to cause a kid who's gone
through *that* to wilt."

Anne touched me—it was the first time in months. "He

glanced towards us; he heard us. He can't be completely out."

"Do you have any objections to a little light hypnosis?"

She looked at the boy. "No. It can't do him any harm now."

I reached out my hand towards his face. His cheek ticked in the shadow of my palm, but when my fingertips only brushed his eyes a line in his throat relaxed. I kept stroking his eyes and whispering to him quietly.

"Okay, open your eyes, 'Frank Baron, Jr.' "

His small black eyes opened.

"Is that really your name?" I asked him.

"I guess so. That's what they call me."

"What's your father's name?"

"Daddy." He snickered; he was making fun of me.

"No stalling. What's his legal name. You're old enough to know that."

His eyebrows jerked up towards his hairline in stages, his breathing came more rapidly. "I don't. I don't know."

"Temporary amnesia," Anne suggested. "He's had a middling bad shock."

"Could be," I admitted reluctantly. "Look, kid, you remember if you *have* a father. Is he alive?"

The eyes went wide. "Look out! *Look out!*"

The boy must be remembering how his father had died, I decided. Yet he didn't seem to be in a state of recall. He seemed to be looking at me and seeing me; and something else.

I ducked and the blast seared right across the kid's blankets, scorching them to rust. The only thing I could see out of the perimeter of my sight was a hand with a gun in it, inserted through the door.

Moving like a sidewinder, I made the threshold and slid the door shut fast, past the safety ease, on the wrist of the gun hand. Fingers exploded apart and the weapon dropped into my own palm. But then the hand wiggled out of the crack; the door came shut, and, infuriatingly latched.

By the time I had used my key the corridor was empty. There was no need to notify Eddie Valesq's security guards. They were on a constant alert, specially since the threats had begun in earnest.

I was finally realizing how deadly earnest those threats had been.

"Are you all right?" I asked Anne. It was a silly question; she had never been in the line of fire.

"Fine." Her face was flushed and for once her hair was disarrayed.

"How's the boy?"

"He's all right. The blast never touched him, only the bedclothes. He seems in natural sleep."

I nodded. "I can see. With a smile on his face. The last thing he saw was somebody getting ready to shoot me in the back."

"But he warned you."

I snorted. "Instinctively. But he thinks that it fortunately wasn't in time."

"You don't think he is your son—or some Frank Baron's son from another probability track."

"No. I think he's my father, from our past."

"And you hate him," Anne said. "You never told me why you hated your father. Why did you?"

"Why does any boy hate his father? I didn't want to, but he made me—he hated me. Wait, I'll tell you about it. My grandfather and his only son both fell in love with the same girl. Old man Baron, the inventor of the probability warp, was only about forty, a widower, and the son was half that. The son married the girl, my mother, and against medical advice, they decided to have a child— me. My mother died. Grandfather blamed my father—my father blamed me. I never found out who Mother had a grudge against."

"Your grandfather left you the business and the invention."

"Of course. After Dad died. He wouldn't let him benefit from anything, even through me. We lived in what used to be Hell's Kitchen. The name still fits. In the closing years of his life, Dad became what might be described as a sadist. I was handy."

"Frank, I know you pretty well. You couldn't be planning on taking out revenge on a boy who would become your father."

"Why not?" I asked. "He couldn't appreciate things the way I did if he was full grown, could he?"

"You have ten minutes left before midnight," Dr. Tan Eck said, seating himself across my desk. "Do you have your decision for me so soon?"

"Yes, Doctor. I have three appointments for midnight and I think I may as well give you the courtesy of hearing my answer first."

"I warn you again, Mr. Baron—refuse me, and I'll go straight to the faxsheets and the government."

"There should be a government agent here shortly, Tan Eck. One of my associates, Miss Tremaine, has been systematically losing him in the esoteric corridors of this building; but he should have located one of his own spies by now who will lead him here."

"Am I going to have to file a complaint with him?" The young scientist smiled charmingly.

"That's your choice. However, Luck, Inc. is *not* going to help you. Your application is refused. We believe unleashing magic in the modern world is not in the public interest."

"There's no such provision in the Warp Bill!" Tan Eck ranted. "If there were, who's to interpret it? You've set yourself up as judge, jury, censor, guardian of public morals. You're a *scoundrel,* Baron."

"True enough. But not a killer like you."

Tan Eck leaned back, his face entirely transparent. He was an emotional man. "What do you mean?" he said calmly enough.

"You had to be the man who tried to shoot me, the one who has probably been threatening me as the Assassin," I said. "I trust the people who work with me—except the spies—and I know from my own spies that the government isn't out to kill me, not just now. Who could get in a place as well guarded as this, and find me, and escape? Somebody with an astronomical amount of luck, a fortune-prone like you—the most pronounced specimen of the breed I've ever known."

"That might all be true," Tan Eck admitted, "but that still doesn't give you the authority to refuse my application for Warp aid."

"I think it does. Listen, Doctor, I don't know whether you know it or not, but your machine—this 'Producer', without all the magic-mumbo—is an illegal patent violation of the Probability Warp! That's what we practice here—magic. At least that's what it would have been called once. But we can't use it indiscriminately, not the way you want to. It has to be used sparingly, under strict supervision."

Tan Eck's lips were thin and his eyes wide. "Under *your* supervision, Baron. Yes! I knew what I had found . . ."

"By luck," I interjected politely.

" . . . By my unique genius, and I knew what you were doing with it. You see, I entirely agree with you—the world can't stand magic, not even a little bit when that magic is controlled by one man. Either all must have it or none."

"Preferably none?"

"Yes, I think it is better if the device—Producer—Probability Warp—is suppressed as completely as poison gas or bacteriological warfare."

"I'm sure you do," I told him. "Not because, as a scientist, you can't stand to see your basic belief in cause and effect violated; not because, as a lover of freedom, you can't stand to see 'magical' powers in the hands of one man; but because if everybody or even one man has this device, he can be luckier than you are. And you've been luckier than everybody else all your life. You can't stand a threat to that—that's why you want to kill me."

Tan Eck's eyes looked much the same as the boy's had earlier.

I coughed discreetly. "Before you reach for that spy-proofed gun, doctor, I might point out to you that with all your luck, you have never pulled off what might be properly described as a miracle. There are a *large* number of guns focused directly on you."

"Believe him, Tan Eck," Eddie Valesq's voice intoned.

"I expected that," he said numbly. "I knew that I would probably get killed murdering you, but there would be a chance, I thought. I'd *certainly* die, wouldn't I?"

"You would. Now get up and get out. Don't try using that invention of yours. If you do, I'll sue you for something as mundane as patent infringement. With more experience at manipulating probability, and even more money than you, I'm bound to win."

He nodded. "I think you would. I feel somehow my luck's run out. It might be better to let your men kill me as I try to kill you. But there's just a chance it wouldn't."

Prince came in as Tan Eck shuffled out.

"Your other midnight appointment," he said.

"Two others, Mr. Prince. Now for the third—LINC rejects your application for Warp aid. Conflict of interests."

"You have no other political party as a client. None of them want to risk being changed by the ethical provisions."

"But we have a client who *doesn't* want an anti-LINC party to get into power. Ourselves—our public relations department hires us to work for our own interest. I think I remembered there was such a thing as self-interest when somebody was trying to kill me."

"This won't look good for you in the news," Prince said narrowly. "I intend to fight you every step of the way, Baron."

"Fine, Mr. Prince. I am a dangerous man; it's absolutely essential that there is somebody to fight me every step of the way."

Prince hesitated, then nodded briefly and left.

Eddie Valesq and Anne entered through a private passage.

"The government man is with the boy. He seems better; he's conscious; but he's still blank. They'll be trouble." Anne was worried.

"There won't be any evidence for trouble. I'm having Wilmot send the boy back where he came from."

"Is there a way back?" Eddie demanded.

"Of course. I've known that all along. Wilmot has been too cocky. He's holding out on me for personal gain. Technological advances come fast in this age—nobody could work on what amounts to refinement of an existing process and not come up with some kind of an answer in twenty years."

"Then you don't want any revenge on the boy?" Anne said, almost happily.

I grinned. "I'm getting plenty of revenge. I'm sending him right back to grow up and go through hell."

"You can't do that to your own father," she protested.

"Listen, Frank, we don't know that anything like a time paradox exists. Why can't Eddie and I raise him here? I can guarantee Eddie isn't going to want his girl when he grows up."

I exhaled. "All right. I have to tell you the rest of it. I tried to shut myself off from the kind of life I went through as a kid, and I succeeded pretty well. But I've had to think about it lately. I grew up in a tough neighborhood. My name was the same as my father's, but could I call myself 'Franklyn Baron the Third.' Not if I didn't want kids to beat my pants off to see if they had lace on them. I was 'Junior Baron'. That kid is *me,* from the past."

"We would still like to keep him here, Frank," Eddie said for the two of them. "Maybe you and he are different. You had to go through all that but maybe he doesn't."

"But he does!" I snarled. "Don't you two idiots see! In some world—probably this one—that kid is going to grow up to be me and run Luck, Inc. He has to go through the same horrible childhood and early life as I did—he has to be the same dictatorial, opinionated, egotistical, power-mad, well-meaning human monster I am. Because if the Probability Warp—Luck, Inc.—*magic* ever falls under the control of anybody soft enough to be sane, this world is washed up. Take a peep at the alternate universes where that's happened. This may not be the best of all possible worlds with me in it, but believe me when I modestly state that it becomes the worst of all possible worlds with *me—this* me—out of it."

They didn't say anything. But then I could always control them easily.

"Will one of you get me some coffee?" I said. "I think I'd better start work early this morning."

RIPENESS

by M. C. Pease

PHILLIP REYNOLDS sat slumped in a chair in the room that served him both as office and living-room. His eyes were tired and his mouth bitter as he watched the televised scene on the wall before him. The picture was of the trial even then going on in the bleak building not very far away. A man was weeping his penitence at daring to think that Marcus, the Director, was less than ideal. It was a horrible spectacle to Phillip. The man would die, executed as a public enemy. But the worst was the knowledge this gave that drugs and torture could so destroy the man's self-respect as to make him beg thus publicly for death. And the thing that made Phillip's soul writhe was the knowledge that he, himself, had been the kingmaker for Marcus.

Director of the World, Marcus was; omnipotent despot over all mankind. And why? Because he, Phillip, had given Marcus the power to bring order where there had been none. "Matilda," they called her, the tool whose making had been Phillip's life. Matilda, because, like a maiden aunt, she was obsessed with details, gathering together the stray threads of gossip and hazy information to build herself a picture of the world. A thing of steel and tungsten and rare elements mixed in a crazy network. A maze of incomprehensible detail, through which small pulses of electricity deftly wove their way—each carrying one small unit of trivial information. A computer, gathering in the news of the world; noting the death of Wong How and the birth of John Smith; observing that Jose Riccardo had lost his job, and that Joe Grundy had bought a refrigerator. The data to organize a world and to save the world from chaos.

Without Matilda, the Decade of Chaos would have been a Century unless the dissolution of anarchy had stopped it sooner; with it, Marcus had first organized his own home-country, the Western States. Then, using the Computer as a tool of empire, he had mediated the argument between Eastern America and Canada, and ended up with both of them in his control. Then he had moved on, with a skill that was not his own, settling quarrels, offering hope, and becoming director of the world. He had given peace; he had given freedom from starvation and from uncertainty; he had controlled the unknown winds of economic fortune. And if, with it, he had also brought slavery, Marcus, at least, felt this was only right.

For Phillip Reynolds, watching the telecast of the trial, the moral question was not answered: had it been right to give this weapon to Marcus? Reynolds had not wondered what the results would be; he had always known. And yet, it had seemed to him there were no alternatives other than tyranny or anarchy. Without control there could only have been collapse; and for control there had to be a strong man, a director. It was a terrible price to pay for time, but it had seemed to Reynolds that mankind must have time at any price.

And yet, he wondered.

His brother did not think so. Peter Reynolds was quite sure that nothing was worth the price, and he had been most bitter in telling Phillip his opinion. Five years ago, that had been. Phillip still remembered that evening, and his brother's unyielding contempt. He had tried to explain; he had tried then, and often since—but never had gotten even a flicker of answering understanding. And finally he had stopped. He had given up going to Stilton University where Peter taught. He had stopped trying, but he had not ever stopped wishing things were different between them. And he had not stopped wondering who was right—Phillip or Peter.

The door burst open to shatter his meditations; Selma and Dirk came tumbling in. These two always amused him, even when they irritated him. But Reynolds could see in each of them some part of himself—himself as he had been, thirty years ago when Matilda had been only a dream. It somehow described himself, he thought, that these two were the mirrored images of that almost-forgotten youth, and yet that they could not get along with each other.

He thought of Selma as the mirror of his heart. This was odd; her specialty was philosophy, though her title only called her his special assistant. Philosophy was supposed to be a cold and unemotional subject; but, then, with Selma, it was far from cold and unemotional. She brought an intense and passionate belief to it; to her, the reign of Marcus the Director was a purgatory for mankind, something to be endured for the sake of a world to be built when it was over. Phillip cherished this dream of an ultimate answer.

Dirk, on the other hand, was a semanticist and cyberneticist. More clearly than anyone, even Phillip, he understood the flow of information through the Computer. And scientists, too, are supposed to be cold, but he was not. He loved Matilda, quite literally. And whatever Matilda might make of the world, however she might be used, was irrelevant before the Computer's perfection.

The two of them, Selma and Dirk, were hardly able to nod to each other without fighting.

"Boss," Selma spat out, "this is it. I quit; I resign. Not you or all the lousy secret police can make me do another lick of work here." She bounced into a chair and looked grim.

Phillip raised an eyebrow at her and half grinned. Then he looked at Dirk. "What's the matter with her?" he asked.

Dirk shrugged. "I don't know; she's gone bats. As far as I know there's nothing new."

"Look," Selma cut in, "this is our chance, the best chance in a long time. Only we got to move fast. And this fool won't do it."

"Do you think it might help if I knew what you were talking about?" Reynolds asked.

The girl looked surprised, then she smiled. "Sorry," she chuckled. "I guess I'm not making much sense. It's the Thorndike cell that Matilda picked up six months ago."

Phillip knew what she was talking about. The Computer handled an enormous amount of quite trivial data, but the pieces often fitted together in very non-trivial ways. In particular, they often added up to conspiracy, the pattern of revolution. To build their revolution, people had to do things; word of what they did was fed into Matilda, and she could then deduce their purpose. The Secret Police did not know this; no one at the Computer had bothered to tell them, and the outward channels were blocked so that the information could be had only on the control boards inside the Computer. But at those boards, each separate group that tried for revolution could be, and was, followed by interested people. The "Thorndike Cell," named for the first person identified as a part of it, was one such group.

"I don't want anything to happen to them," Selma continued. "They're not like the usual bunch of neurotic troublemakers that make up most cells. These people are decent folk, and they have brains, too. College teachers, professional people. The kind that really can build a new world. They're not just revolting *against,* but they're working *for* what they believe in. They're different, and I don't want to see them squashed."

"Who's squashing them?" Phillip asked. "Dirk?"

"No." She was contemptuous. "It's the police; according to Matilda, the police are getting suspicious, beginning to track them down." It would have interested the Secret Police—interested them greatly—to know how much about them Matilda could deduce.

"Oh? And what do you want Dirk to do? Or not do?" Phillip asked.

She leaned forward. "Help them! You can do it. Matilda's got the power, enormous power. Just juggle the figures a bit. Make other people do things that will throw the police off. I don't know what; you guys are the experts on Matilda. You tell me. But do something."

"I keep telling her there's nothing we can do," Dirk said in an exasperated voice. "The Computer either works, or she doesn't; and if she doesn't, the roof falls in— complete and utter chaos. Sure, I'd like to help them; but I don't want to upset the world for the sake of a handful of people with ideals."

"There must be some way," Selma cried. "The Computer's too powerful for there not to be a way to use it."

"No," Dirk drawled. "The cobalt bomb is powerful, too, but there's no way you can use it without using all of its power. Sure, we could shut down the Computer. Then Marcus and the entire Directory would be so busy trying to keep the world from collapsing, they'd have no time at all for a little thing like a conspiracy. So we burn down the house to light our cigarette; that's not what we want."

"I'm afraid Dirk's right," Reynolds said, and his voice was sad. "At least, I don't know of any way to get the Computer to juggle things just a little bit. It's either all or none; and I don't think even you want that." He wished there were something he could do. He felt the guilt that lay upon him for the original decision he had made, to be Marcus' tool; but Phillip did not know what he could do now.

"Then I quit." The girl's lips were thin. "It's time to stand up or shut up, and I'm not going to sit in here like a mouse and watch the mighty Marcus sit in sated power. I'm going out and get me a job where I can help the revolution; maybe I'll go to Stilton U. and find the Thorndike group itself."

Phillip sat up straight with a start. "Stilton University? Is that . . .? My brother, is he in this?"

Selma gazed at him with wide eyes. "I don't know," she said. "I never thought."

Phillip jumped to his feet, and strode across the room. Pushing back the curtains that hung there, he switched on the lights of the control-board that the curtains had concealed. It was a simple-looking thing. Three small cathode ray screens; a few colored lights; a typewriter without keys and one with keys; and a battery of numbered buttons—that was all. But it was the main control-board of the vast Computer that was Matilda. Reynolds sat down in the chair before it, and turned a switch that gave it life.

Phillip moved with practiced speed. One hand, on the panel of buttons, punched out a coded sequence. A screen responded, lighting with a symbol to describe its interpretation of that sequence; the machine was ready to receive a query. Another sequence and another symbol. It recognized the authority of the interrogator to ask questions it would not otherwise have answered. A third sequence and the area of questioning was defined. Revolution. A fourth, and it was narrowed to the Thorndike cell. Only then did Reynolds move to the keyed typewriter and type, *"Probable present composition and percentage of probable assurance. Query."* The second typewriter, the one without keys, typed the question with him, then spaced to give the answer.

The wait was too short to be noticeable by human observation, but it began to type the answer—before Phillip's eyes, the list of names grew. But all he saw was the one in second place: *"Second in command—Peter Reynolds—93 per cent."* There was shock on his face as he sat there staring at it. His brother, second-in-command! And with an assurance of 93 per cent that this was true!

It was a long moment after the typewriter had stopped that Phillip bent forward again and typed: *"Repeat conditions. Probable present plans of revolutionary nature and percentage of probable assurance. Query."* And the second typewriter answered: *"Second query. Assassination of Marcus while leaving the Anniversary Celebration. 78 per cent."*

Phillip's face was dead as he typed again: *"Repeat conditions. Further second query. Probability of success. Query."* His face did not move as he read the answer: *"Third query. 0.8 per cent."* And still his face was cold as he typed: *"Repeat conditions. Probability of arrest of Peter Reynolds within one year from present. Query."* But his eyes blinked as he saw the answer: *"Fourth query. 98.6 per cent."*

Once more Phillip moved to ask the machine a question: *"Repeat conditions. Further fourth query. Probability of arrest of Peter Reynolds prior to action noted response second query. Query."* He smiled slightly as the other typewriter answered: *"Fifth query. 3.4 per cent."* At least his brother was not apt to be arrested before the Celebration.

His hand looked as if it moved of its own intent as it punched out on the buttons the sequence to switch off the board. The man himself seemed in a state of shock.

There were two weeks before the Anniversary Celebration in honor of the final union of the whole world in the slavery of Marcus. Two weeks of grace; two weeks of life for Peter. That was all. If anything could be done, there was only two weeks in which to do it.

II

After sitting hunched for several minutes, Phillip Reynolds got up and started pacing back and forth. Selma looked at him; then she looked at Dirk and got up herself. "I guess this isn't the time to press my resignation. Anyway, he's all stirred up, which is what I wanted to do anyway. So let's get out of here." Dirk nodded, a sardonic expression in his eyes. He wondered if he should point out that it was not her threat to quit that had stirred Phillip up; it had taken the knowledge that Peter was in danger to do it. But he shrugged, mentally. Selma was not a girl to try to fool herself, and he doubted if it would be an effective taunt. So, without saying anything, he just followed her out.

It was about a minute later that the door opened again and Rance came in. Rance Kirsten was huge—in width at least. A vast mountain of a man with a face that rarely showed emotion, and whose eyes seemed perpetually hidden beneath rolls of flesh. He sighed slightly as he lowered himself carefully into a chair. He did not like exertion and, in fact, rarely even left his room.

Phillip nodded at him vaguely. He knew Kirsten as a remarkable man, thinking of him as an extension of the Computer, for Rance had a strange faculty of intuition. The fat man, he knew, spent his time sprawled in a comfortable chair watching a large screen he had had built into one wall of his room. Across that screen moved the data being carried on various channels that Rance selected, apparently at random. How much of the information Kirsten absorbed, Phillip did not know; but he did know that out of it Rance somehow synthesized an awareness of the future that even the Computer could not give.

"Hi," the big man grunted. "Thought you might want to talk to me." Phillip looked at him in surprise. It was true; he did want to talk to Rance—but he had not known it until now. And how had Rance known? He shrugged, and rapidly told the other what the problem was. "And what do I do now?" he ended.

Rance blinked. "What do you want to do?" he asked.

"Well," Phillip said slowly, his face furrowed with thought, "I want to save my brother, of course. He's eight years younger than me, you know; I guess I got in the habit of taking care of him when we were kids. But there's more than that. He's an idealist; thinks people should be free, and that Marcus is about the worst thing that ever happened to the world. He's never forgiven me for letting Marcus use the Computer to build his empire. And the worst of it is that he may be right.

"I thought mankind needed a strong hand to do the reorganizing that had to be done. I thought it needed time, and that even Marcus was not too high a price to pay for time. But I'm not sure, and Peter could be right that that's too high a price for anything. If he is right, and if he dies for his beliefs, then I'm the one who killed him, for it's I who gave Marcus his power." There was a bitter twist to his mouth and he paced back and forth for a minute in silence.

"And there's more, too," Reynolds finally continued. "I never thought of Marcus as more than a temporary answer. But he's too strong. Eventually, I suppose, he'll fall; if it's a slow dissolution, or if it comes by the chaos of revolution, what happens then? What comes after? Do we go back to chaos and wars and economic turbulence? Maybe it's up to me to do something; maybe if I don't, the time I've bought will go for nothing. But what can I do?" He turned to the fat man, desperation on his face.

"You know," Rance said, his voice low, "we talk a lot about revolution in here. When do you suppose they're going to arrest us for it?"

Phillip looked at him in surprise. "Us?" He was however, almost used to Rance's wandering methods of discussion. "Oh, they won't arrest us; they tried to several years ago. We had a big argument. Told them I wouldn't stand for it, and convinced them I meant it. They knew they needed the Computer and that there wasn't anybody else could run it. So, there was a lot of face-saving, but it kind of worked out that they don't come in here, and we don't go out there."

He smiled, remembering that period. Vane, the head of the Secret Police, had writhed in frustration; he had panted and fumed and roared. But in the end, confronted with Reynolds' unwavering logic, he had collapsed into sullen silence. And quietly Phillip had built his walls, using the full talents of some very smart people, and of the Computer, to keep Vane from ever getting knowledge of what went on inside the sanctuary of the Computer building.

"So you don't think they find out what goes on here?" Kirsten asked. "Well, maybe they don't; but if I were Vane, I'd at least have my spies in here; wouldn't you?"

"Sure," Phillip shrugged. "He probably does. Only they can't send word out; all they can do is walk out themselves, and then we don't let them back. So their spies don't do them much good."

"No," Rance agreed. "Except that if we started actively plotting, then that would be news that it would be worth sacrificing a spy for, wouldn't it? So it seems like it's kind of a stalemate between us and Vane, doesn't it?"

"You mean that we're safe as long as we don't start mixing in?" Phillip swung toward the fat man, a puzzled look on his face. "Sure. But so what? That's what I pointed out to Vane long ago, and you must have known this." He paused, and then his face lit up. "Or are you just reminding me?" Suddenly he drooped. "But that is true. There's nothing I can do; any funny stuff and I cut our own throats."

Rance heaved himself out of his chair and waddled to the door. After he had opened it, he turned and looked back at Phillip. "Nothing wrong with 'funny stuff.' The only thing you can't do is plot. Subtlety—that's what you got to avoid like the poison." He started to swing around, but stopped and looked back again. "One other thing. A piece of information for you that you can't get from Matilda. Marcus is strong now, as strong as he's going to get. From here out it's a downward road for him, a fight to hold what he's got, and he probably knows it." This time he did leave, closing the door gently as Phillip started to ask him some more questions.

Staring at the closed door, Phillip asked himself questions. What, he wondered, had Rance been driving at? He wished he understood the man better; sometimes it seemed as if the man enjoyed being cryptic. Maybe he did. Anyway, it seemed clear that Kirsten did have some idea of what might be done. From his last words, it almost sounded as if he thought this was the ideal time. But ideal for what? That was the question. What could be done? Selma wanted to juggle the Computer so that it would give false answers—not false enough to worry Marcus or his people, but just enough to give the revolutionists a break. Dirk did not think it could be done. For himself, Reynolds was sure it could not be. Not by changing the orders to the Computer or juggling its codes. Perhaps it could be accomplished by cutting into the transmission lines, to put in false information and wrong orders. But that would take activity, and Kirsten had pointed out that that would be sure suicide. No, Rance must have some other answer, and Phillip could not think what it might be.

It was late at night, after many hours of intense concentration, that Reynolds finally thought he saw the light. He was frightened at the answer. It would be he who took the risk of it, and if it failed, it would be he who paid the penalty by starring in the next big trial. But it did seem to have a chance of working.

He started to pick up the phone to call Rance, and maybe Selma and Dirk, but he stopped. It would be far better if none of them knew what he planned. Safer for them, and perhaps even safer for him and for his plan. And maybe that had been in Kirsten's mind, too—that he should not tell the exact details. Maybe Rance had some good reason for not wanting to know the details. No, it was his show, alone, Phillip Reynolds decided; and he would have to do it alone.

After once more going over his plan in detail, Phillip finally sat down in the chair of the Computer control unit. His fingers flew, and symbols danced across the screen in answer to his questions and his orders. Twice he checked his results to make sure there was no error in what he had done; and then, very carefully, he erased the record of what he had done. With a final checking of the results, he nodded in satisfaction and closed down the unit.

Moving to the phone-box he pushed the button and spoke a series of numbers. The voice that answered him was cold and impersonal. "Let me speak to Vane," Phillip said. The voice answered him: "Mr. Vane is not available." There was the barest accent on the title. Reynolds made his voice equally cold. "This is Phillip Reynolds; I wish to speak to Vane. You will please inform him." There was a moment's silence, and then the voice accepted, and asked him to hold the line.

It was a full minute before he heard Vane's rasping voice: "Vane here." Phillip leaned forward, his eyes glazed with concentration, his voice slow and careful: "Mr. Vane, I have matters of considerable importance to communicate. Will you please arrange an appointment for me and yourself with Marcus in the morning."

"What are these matters?" the Police Commissioner asked.

"That I will explain tomorrow," Phillip said; "not to-night." He tried to put finality in his voice.

"You will tell me what you know," Vane said, "and I will be the one to decide if it is a matter for Marcus' ear."

"That is impossible," Reynolds answered. "Actually, this is not a Police matter. I would, however, like to have you present when I discuss it with Marcus. If you don't care to cooperate, I shall have to proceed without you. This will take longer, of course, and time is very short. However, I am prepared to accept this delay if you insist; if you do, I believe you will ultimately regret your decision."

He smiled and his eyes glinted as, after a moment's pause, he went on: "You will also remember that, through the Computer, I have access to knowledge that you do not. What I will discuss with Marcus is based on that knowledge. It is not, however, directly concerned with revolution. I do not expect, for example, to mention your connection with the man known as Rimaldi."

All of the people high in service of Marcus had their

own hidden connections, as the Computer had deduced. Rimaldi, a powerful man in the underworld, was Vane's chief ace-in-the-hole. "I would prefer, as I say, to have you there, but it is not really essential." A little blackmail Phillip thought, might get results.

Vane was quiet for a moment. When he did speak, his voice was carefully controlled, giving no sign of what he might be feeling. "Very well, Reynolds, I will see what I can do." The light on the box went out, indicating the connection was broken.

He had won his point, Phillip knew; Vane was perhaps the one man in all the world who could always get to see Marcus on request. Not that Marcus trusted him; quite the contrary. But Marcus trusted no one else, and Vane was the one most likely to bring him news of the others.

So now, Phillip thought, he was committed. This was the point beyond which there was no possibility of withdrawal. Vane knew now that something was afoot, and he would not rest until he knew what that something was. Now, whether his plan was good or bad, he must go through with it.

The next morning, in answer to Vane's summons, Phillip called a car and left the Computer building. Not having been outside the building for better than six months, he stopped a moment at the door to breathe unfiltered air, and to remember the feel of wind on his cheek.

As he stepped to the car, two men fell in a step behind him, one on each side. They did not say anything, and neither did Reynolds. He was not surprised; this was routine whenever he left the sanctuary of the building. And when he got in the car, one of them sat beside him, while the other sat beside the driver.

At the door to the private offices of Marcus, he was, according to custom, made to strip and then examined with X-ray and with other instruments. Finally donning the silk robes provided for all guests, and noting with his usual amusement how skillfully they were designed to hamper motion, he was admitted to the anteroom. Vane was already there, dressed in a similar robe, standing in the center of the room looking impassive.

The Police Commissioner gave him a hard look and

a nod. Probably, Reynolds thought, Vane would love to ask him questions but did not dare since the room was no doubt well equipped with listening devices. Phillip sat down in a chair and prepared to wait.

It was not a long wait, as these things went. About an hour and a quarter, Phillip noted, before a man opened a door and nodded to them to come in. They entered side by side, pacing off in measured steps the carpet that led up the long hall toward the desk at its end. That desk was the only furniture in the room. On the walls, there were maps of the world, and overhead there were the patterns of the constellations. Did that mean, Phillip wondered, that Marcus claimed the allegiance, not only of the world but of the stars as well? But he did not let the smile that was in his mind show on his face.

III

The desk itself was so big as to dwarf the man behind it; and yet, you could not ignore the man—for there was a magnetism to him that commanded all attention. His eyes were dark and brooding, deepset in his hawk-like face. The mouth was a grim slit that turned down at the corners. The man himself was probably small. He did not often let himself be seen standing, but his shoulders were broad and he looked powerful; and his hands were big and brutal. He looked at Vane.

The two of them gave the conventional salute, and then Vane spoke: "Sir, this man, Phillip Reynolds, who is Operating Chief of the Computer, has requested this interview. With your permission, I will let him speak."

The director's eyes gleamed with malice. "You mean you don't know why he's here?" His voice was deep and resonant, an excellent speaking voice. "What kind of a hold does he have over you? No matter; we will hear what he has to say." And he looked over towards Phillip.

"Marcus, sir," Phillip said, hesitating just a moment to collect his thoughts, "you stand now as the ruler of the entire world. Under you, the world has learned to live in peace, without fear of hunger or of the cold; you will be recorded in history as the man who has achieved what no man has done before. Napoleon, Bismarck, Hitler,

Stalin, these and others had the same dream as you. But they failed, and you have succeeded."

Marcus nodded slightly. "This I know; are you flattering me, or are you leading up to something?"

"Marcus, sir, I am trying to say that you now stand at a turning point. Because you have succeeded, you have an opportunity before you that no man has ever had before." He paused, but the director said nothing, only looked at him with guarded eyes. "A man who accomplishes so much as you have, must act in that accomplishment against the dreams of many other men. These other men are little people; perhaps you do not think them worth considering—and perhaps they are not. And yet, it is the irony of history that it is those same small people—or their children—who will judge you; it is they who will determine the name that you will carry through the coming centuries."

"You are long-winded, Mr. Reynolds," the director said. "What are you proposing?"

"Marcus, sir," Phillip answered, "you are now at the peak of your power. Nothing remains for you to do except to fight to hold that power. Unless . . . Unless you use that power to build the future of mankind."

"I was under the impression," Marcus said, his voice dry, "that I had already built that future; did you not say so yourself?"

"Marcus, sir," Phillip hesitated, to choose his words with care, "I have said that you have built an empire of the world. But you, sir, must know better than anyone else that you have not yet built the future; that will be built by your lieutenants. Sarno has the army. It is his; so much is official.

"But you must also know that seventeen percent of that army does not exist, and that the money so diverted is used to finance his own spy system.

"Lemark has the industry of the world; this, too, is official. But steel and other industries report no profit, and that is false. And the profits that are not there, are used for arms hidden near his labor camps; this, too, you must know. And Vane, I am sure, will confirm my words."

He looked at the Police Commissioner who stared back

at him impassively. Phillip shrugged and went on: "Ferrar, Richards, Berrin, and the others. These are smaller men and their opportunities are more limited. But each has a similar story.

"Where is your future there, Marcus, sir? You balance their powers, playing this one against that. You are a master of this juggling. But someday you will weaken. Someday you will grow tired or bored. What then, Marcus, sir? I am quite confident, sir, that you know better than anyone else what uncertainty there lies in the future."

The director's face was completely impassive. "And what, Mr. Reynolds," he said, "are you proposing that I do?"

Phillip bit his lip, and his eyes shifted for a moment, but then he straightened up. "Marcus, sir, I am proposing that you do what no other dictator has ever done. Others have risen when the time was ripe for strong personal rule, and organization; some have honestly believed that what they did was for the ultimate good of mankind. But none have been able to relinquish power when that time was ripe, and because they wouldn't, all they built decayed within a generation or less—where it was not destroyed in the wars they invoked in order to retain their power.

"I am proposing, Marcus, sir, that you go farther than they did—that you earn yourself the title in history of the man who not only unified the world, and saved it from chaos—but also of the man who unified it in freedom and in love. It would be a wonderful thing, sir, if, at your Anniversary Celebration, while acknowledging the acclaim of the world, you should also announce that you would, six months from thence, resign your leadership in favor of a democracy of the world. And that you were even then calling together a congress of the world's thinkers to devise a constitution for that democracy. This, sir, would be a wonderful thing, and one that would truly earn you a unique place in history."

The director smiled slightly while he thought a moment. Then he looked at the Police Commissioner. "Vane," he said, "our friend here is suffering from a surfeit of idealism. I think he needs a rest, and perhaps a bit of treatment. Will you see to it? But," he held up his hand, "nothing violent. When he is cured, I shall expect him to continue to run his Computer, so, be careful. Cure him, but don't kill him."

"Yes, sir." Vane smiled, and it was a grim smile. And grasping Phillip's arm, he turned the Computer man around and marched him out a side door.

Reynolds, feeling that implacable hand on his arm, trembled at what lay ahead. He had no illusions of what the "cure" might mean; he had no illusions at all about the nature of the police state that was the world under Marcus. And yet, there was also gladness in his heart. Now he was not only committed to the plan—his plan— but he was actually started on it. Now the dice were cast, and rolling to their destined end.

And there was something more. In himself Phillip Reynolds recognized some certain masochistic pleasure at the thought of what lay before him. There was a sense of satisfaction in it, a feeling of ultimate justice. It was he who had made Marcus—quite deliberately, and with full knowledge of what he was doing. It was, in a sense, irrelevant that he had created the director only to save the world, that Reynolds still believed that there had been no other way to save humanity. People had suffered because of it. They had died; their souls had been tortured and drugged out of them, their pride destroyed with malice. It was fitting that he should suffer in his turn, even in the act of retribution.

And Peter. Peter did not believe in him; his brother thought him a traitor to humanity, and had rejected him. There was an irony in the thought that he should be made to suffer to save the boy from the folly of a doomed revolt. And Phillip was amused to think that by and in this act, he hoped to prove that Peter was wrong.

He was afraid, but also he was other things.

IV

It was the morning of the fifth day that Phillip Reynolds was taken out of the bleak building where he had spent those five eternities, and was brought to a waiting car. When the car had brought him to the Computer building, the guards were not gentle as they pulled him out. And when, finally, they shoved him through the door of what had been his own office, they took positions just inside with guns held ready in their fists.

Through eyes that could not focus well, he saw that Vane was seated in his favorite chair. The main people of his group were standing uneasily along the opposite wall—Selma, Dirk, Rance Kirsten, Henry Cortson of Maintenance, Ralph Martin of Personnel, Jim Coster of Purchasing. Behind the Police Commissioner were several uniformed men, quite undistinguished except by the brutality of their faces.

Phillip straightened up and threw a smile at his own people. Then he nodded curtly at the policeman. "Hi, Vane. Or must I now say Mr. Vane?"

"I don't care what you call me," the other said, his voice rasping harshly. "Just do the job you're here for. Or else."

Phillip opened up his mouth to answer when there was a sudden commotion at the door behind him. He turned to see it swing open and two men in the uniform of Marcus' own guard enter. Behind them were two others. The first pair stalked across the room where they turned to look with hard eyes around the room. The second two stayed near the door. "Mr. Vane," one of them said, his voice cold and impersonal. "You will have your men leave; they may find a nearby room to wait."

Vane was startled. Then he jumped to his feet and motioned his men out with a jerk of his head.

There was a moment's pause while the room waited with quick breath; then suddenly two more uniformed men came in, these with their guns in their hands. At their signal, the other guards drew their guns. Then Marcus entered and quietly sat down in the chair. He nodded at Vane's salute and said: "I was told you had brought Mr. Reynolds here. I will handle this myself."

"I . . . I . . . Certainly sir." The Commissioner was clearly flabbergasted. "I thought I could handle it myself and did not want to bother you. But I will be most happy to . . ." His voice trailed off.

"It does not matter whether you could or not," the director said. "Without the Computer, the State is in jeopardy, and the affair is certainly worth my own interest."

"I don't really think it's that serious, sir," Vane said. He would have gone on, but the director interrupted him.

"You don't, eh?" Marcus asked. "Look at this." He pulled a paper from his pocket and held it out. "The daily production record of key items that is put on my desk each morning. Do you see what it says? Yesterday, in all the world, there was produced exactly forty-seven pounds of steel. Pounds, mind you. Not mega-tons or even kilo-tons, but pounds! That is the data that the Computer gave me this morning. I've had technicians question over my printer; I thought it was in error. I've had Lemark send me over his own report. It was only this morning that I found that his printer was saying the same thing, and that he was faking up the sheets that he was sending me. It is not the printer that is in error, but the Computer; this is the data that it gives, and it is wrong!

"Do you know what this means? Or are you so engrossed in your own small problems that you cannot think? I tell you that without true data the world will be in chaos in a matter of weeks, maybe less. We cannot live without the Computer, even as you could not live without your nervous system. We could not in the old days; there was war and famine and dissolution.

"Now we are organized, far more highly organized than we ever were before. And, too, we have forgotten how to operate without this tool, even so far as we ever knew. Without the Computer, there can not now be any hope of the survival of our civilization.

"Mr. Vane, this is a *very* serious matter." The director's eyes were hard and tight, and there was a whiplash in his voice.

"Yes, sir, I see, sir. I . . . I'm happy you will take over, sir." Vane was flustered and could not seem to find his balance. "I had just started, sir. Mr. Reynolds came in just the minute before you did, sir; I had been questioning the others. They claim they do not know what the matter is, and . . . that they had been doing everything they could to find and fix it."

"Perhaps," the director agreed. "But I am aware of a strong coincidence, here. Mr. Reynolds comes to me with an idiot plea. I place him in your care, and immediately the Computer breaks down. Coincidence or purpose, Mr. Reynolds?"

Phillip, looking into those cold eyes, felt more afraid than he ever had in his life. But, drawing on his reserves of strength, he took a deep breath and answered: "Marcus, sir, I still believe you have an opportunity before you now that will not come again. I still hope you will take it and release the world for freedom. As to what is the matter with the Computer, I do not know, and I do not think *you* can find out. Coincidence? No, I do not think so. But what are you going to do about it?"

There was a moment's silence, before Marcus, in an almost gentle voice said: "There are ways of finding out, Mr. Reynolds. And I think I have demonstrated in the past my willingness to use those ways."

"Marcus, sir," Phillip answered, "I am aware of that. But consider. You do not have much time; you cannot stand for many days the loss of the Computer. Your directorship will fall into chaos if you do not find the answer fast.

"And consider further: I may or may not have the answer. So may or may not each of these others here. Which of us will you question? This is an important point, and you should study it well, for your methods of obtaining the truth are rough; they depend on drugs or torture. And your methods are so rough that if a person *really* does not know the answer—why, he will give you an answer, anyway. How will you know if the answer you get is the right one?"

"If it is the right one it will work," Marcus said.

Phillip nodded. "That's true; but if it's the wrong one, its trial may do incalculable and irreparable harm. Myself, for instance. Any answer you get from me will be in the form of a coded sequence for the master control board. The code for that board is nowhere written down; I have always considered it too dangerous to write down. And how are you to know that I have not given you the sequence that wipes out all of the Computer's memories?

"If you asked the question wrongly, that might be a good answer; at least it would prevent the Computer from giving wrong answers. But, once done, it could not then be undone; it would take five years to get the Computer back even to where it is now. Could you take that risk? Would you dare to try out any answer I might give you?"

"If I was sure I had the right person, yes." The director's voice was cold and flat.

"That is exactly the question," Phillip said; "but how can you know?" He dared to smile.

"I have a way." Marcus also smiled. "I shall ask Rance."

There was a movement of surprise in all the Computer people. Dirk spun to look at the fat man, his face darkening with understanding and with anger. "So you're a spy." He spat out the words.

The fat man heaved a sigh. "Yes, I am a spy. Matter of fact, I'm his brother." He nodded at Marcus. "Probably other spies here, but I'm Mark's." He waddled over to a chair and sat down. "Glad it's out in the open; now I can sit down." He sighed again, from comfort.

"Well?" Marcus barked. "What's the answer?"

Rance shrugged. "There isn't any. Everybody here is capable of it. They live and dream revolution, here; everybody—except maybe the spies, and they have to pretend. Phillip's in it, no doubt; he's acting from no visible surprise. But it's quite possible he doesn't know what's been done. In fact, if he did not do it, he probably doesn't know. Better way to do things: each man knows only what he has to know. The man you want is the man who actually sabotaged the machine. Could be anyone."

"I think you know," Marcus answered. "Or if you don't know, you could guess. And with your intuition, your guess would probably be right. What's your guess?"

"Won't tell you," Rance said, "because they're right; you're through. Supposing you do break this, find out what's wrong and fix it. Shall I tell you your future? Shall I prophesy just how long you'll last? It's not long.

"Right now you're at the top. But things are building up, and you'll end up in the gutter. Me, I'm a spy, yes. But I'm a spy for you, Mark, not for the directorship; and I'm telling you to be a hero."

"That's up to me to decide." Marcus' voice was tight. "Tell me what you think, or I'll tear you apart to get the answer."

Rance closed his eyes and was silent a moment. When he spoke, his voice was so low as to be almost inaudible. "I am your brother, Mark. I don't like your threatening me; if I thought you meant it, I'd be your enemy. Don't try to prove it to me, because I think I'd be a dangerous enemy for you. You're through, Mark; you're through, regardless of what happens here. The only option you have is how to take it."

The aura of tension in the room was oppressive; Rance's fat, full face, with the eyes still closed, seemed carved from icy rock. Marcus, his face betraying no emotion, but masklike and impervious, was still and brooding. Selma's eyes were wide, and her motions were jerky as she looked from one to the other. Dirk looked pleased as if there were deep laughter inside him at the drama of this scene. The others, each to his temperament and understanding, were fixed in fear or surprise.

Phillip Reynolds felt quite calm, and yet he knew he would not ever remember with any clarity what had happened here; it would seem like a dream, uncertainly recalled. But he was pleased to note that his voice was normal as he asked: "Marcus, sir, which will it be? Will you force chaos, or will you accept the opportunity to be the savior of mankind?"

Phillip's words seemed to break the spell. The director smiled slightly. "Mr. Vane," he asked, "do you concede now that this is an affair somewhat beyond your authority?"

He stood up, not waiting for an answer, and turned to Phillip. "It is your hand, I believe, Mr. Reynolds. I fear you hold all the cards." He smiled a bit more widely. "But the game is still interesting. My friends and staff members will not approve; if they find out, I will not live to become your hero. The challenge of that circumstance is interesting. And afterwards . . . afterwards there will be still further trouble. They will not easily give up the power that they have; I fear that they will have to die."

He walked to the door, and then turned once more. "So that I may live until the Anniversary Celebration, you will all remain within this building. Even you, Rance; and you, Mr. Vane; and your men; and those of my men who are in this room. My other men will guard the door, and they will have orders to kill. Afterwards, when the die is cast, then I will need Mr. Vane; I think he will work for me because he has a good nose for a winning side. And . . . I have no doubt that I will win. You are undoubtably correct that the tide of history is moving."

His eyes were still cold as they swept around the room. "I will expect the Computer to be corrected at a very early time." He turned and walked out.

It was Rance who first moved. He heaved himself to his feet and waddled toward the door. "I will leave when I can," he said. "It is too bad, too, because I have liked it here; but the old order passeth." He went out.

Vane and the other policemen, and the men of Marcus' guard, followed him out; they walked as if in a state of shock, not yet comprehending what had happened.

Henry Cortson, Ralph Martin, and Jim Coster also drifted out, looking stunned but happy. They would drift into the lounge, Phillip thought, to talk it over, trying to make sense out of it all, and wondering what would happen. They would talk about it, he knew, and then gradually drift into active planning; they were good fellows.

They were all good fellows, even Rance. The chap had been a spy—but still, it had been he who had told Phillip this was the time, not for plotting, but for a pure power play. And he had been right; it *had* been the time. The men around Marcus were beginning to jockey for position, each aiming at the pinnacle. Until now, they had been together, fearing the world; but now that they felt the directorship secure, they were beginning to maneuver to seize it for themselves. And Marcus knew this; he knew —though perhaps he had not admitted it to himself—that this would soon destroy his power, and that his days were numbered closely.

And then, too, this was the psychological time. Marcus had conquered the world; the only thing that was left for him to do was to conquer the hearts of men. He could only do that by such an act as they had forced him into.

But whatever the reason, events had proven this was in fact the time to strike. The die had been cast; Phillip had won his bet. And it was Rance who, at the end, had called the score and made the director see it. Phillip would die, he supposed, still wondering what manner of man Rance was.

There was only Selma and Dirk left in the room with Phillip. He looked at them, smiling, wondering what to say that would not be anticlimax. But the girl saved him the problem. "Oh, Phillip," she said, "that was wonderful." And on sudden impulse she bounded over to him and kissed him soundly.

"It certainly was," Dirk chimed in. "Got to hand it to you."

Selma whirled on him. "What are you putting your two bits in for?" she asked. "You dessicated mechanic, you wouldn't lift a finger; in fact, you worked your fool head off trying to repair Matilda. You'd better go crawl into a vacuum tube."

Dirk stared at her. Then with a shrug, he went over to the control panel and his fingers began to fly over the buttons. Having put in the opening sequence, he moved to the typewriter and, apparently, rattled off a series of questions without even looking at the answers. After giving the closing sequence, he ripped out the paper from the other typewriter, glanced at it, nodded once, and tossed it on the table. Then he stalked out without saying anything at all.

Phillip picked it up and read what it said:

"Subject: Coding.

"Information received re steel. Coding number. Query.

"Reply query: 236/648/76.

"Information transmitted re steel. Coding number. Query.

"Reply query: 236/648/75.

"Material whose coding number for receipt of information is the same as that given in response 2nd query. Query.

"Reply 3rd query: Steroid No. 6742.

"End."

Phillip smiled. So that was the material of which only forty-seven pounds had been made the day before; he had wondered. But this was of no significance; what was of profound significance was that Dirk had, by his series of questions to the Computer, shown that he knew exactly what had been done to Matilda. For Phillip Reynolds had simply instructed the Computer to code incoming data one unit higher than normal, and to use the normal code for all other operations. Hence, all the data received had been simply misfiled; and Dirk had known this.

Selma was starting to say something, but Phillip interrupted her. "You are a fool," he said, but his voice was kindly. "Dirk knew what he was doing; he is too good a computerman not to be able to figure out what had happened. This paper proves it. He did not find out what was wrong with Matilda quite simply because he took good care not to."

Selma stared at him with wide eyes. Then, with a little, wordless cry she turned around and darted out the door.

Reynolds laughed. The two of them together would make a good team, once they learned to understand each other. And this time, he thought, they probably would.

It was some eight months later, when all the shooting and the speech-making were over and while the new democracy of the world was still trying to find its feet, that Phillip Reynolds sat down at the counter of a coffee shop where he had found his brother Peter. "Do you mind?" he asked.

Peter looked around at him and looked somewhat surprised, but not very much so. "Hello, Phillip," Peter said. "This is a public place; it does not matter whether I mind or not."

"It does to me," Phillip answered. "I was hoping we could be friends again. After all, the whole situation is changed; the directorship is gone. Marcus is retired, and no one knows where. His cohorts are dead or vanished. Your own group—that we used to call the Thorndike group—is now important in the new government of freedom. And I . . . I am an old man now; I have retired.

"The Computer is being run by Selma and Dirk, Mr. and Mrs. Richards—at least as much as it is run by any individuals. Matilda, which was the tool of Marcus, is now the tool of the New Democracy of the World; and it is just as effective a tool. Without it, your dreams and hopes would have gone for nothing, for the world is too complicated to be run by purely human hands. To make the wise and necessary decisions, far too much data must be integrated. Whether it be under a directorship, or the government of free men, Matilda is the tool to hold off chaos. Don't you understand?"

Peter put down his coffee cup and looked at him with deliberation. "You have built a fine Computer, yes; I never said you didn't. But it takes more than that to make yourself a man.

"You hated Marcus and the things he did; if you had loved him and thought the things he did were right, then I'd have been puzzled, but I'd have conceded you the right to your opinion. But you didn't. You knew he was evil, and you just didn't have the guts to do anything about it; that I cannot forgive." He slid off the stool and turned to walk out.

Phillip opened his mouth to call him back. But what would he say? Tell the truth? He didn't dare; for if the world knew that it was the Computer which had been behind all, then they would never trust it. For Matilda had shown Phillip Reynolds the terrible necessity for Marcus' regime, simply by indicating the devastation and decline which would come unless a world directorship could rule long enough to organize the world. If they knew the power of Matilda, they would destroy her; they would not dare do otherwise.

And, too, if the truth should become known, then the myth that was Marcus would be destroyed. Marcus was now the shining idol, the man who had, with infinite skill and cleverness, forged the freedom of the world. And it was strange, but that myth was already a potent force— perhaps even the most powerful force—for the goal of a free and stable world. To destroy that image, false though it was, would be to undermine the very thing for which Phillip Reynolds had fought.

No, he could not speak; he could not say the words, tell the facts, that would make Peter know what he had done. And it was not important that he had done it partially for Peter, to save his brother from the penalty of what would have been an abortive revolution.

No, his lips were sealed. He and the others would have

to live out their lives, satisfied with only their own knowledge of what they had done.

There was sadness in him as he watched his brother walk out of the coffee house.

THE END

☐ **TERROR,** by Robert Bloch
"A brand-new novel by one of the top suspense writers of our time"—*N. Y. Telegraph.*   #L92-537, 50¢

☐ **I AM TERESA,** by A. R. Dispaldo
The novel of a woman's brazen witchery, and the evil that infected a small New England village.   #91-257, 35¢

☐ **GUN-LAW FOR LAVERCOMBE,** by Charles Alden Seltzer
Killer trained killer to a blazing showdown along the Arizona Trail.
                #91-258, 35¢

☐ **CITIZENS,** by Meyer Levin
Emotion-packed story of a gripping courtroom drama by the author of *Compulsion.* "Remarkable"—*N. Y. Times.*   #L94-538, 75¢

☐ **HOW TO GET ALONG WITH YOUR CHILD,** by Mrs. Shirley Camper
"The book of the year for all parents," by the *Consultant to the Family Service Association of America.*   #L92-539, 50¢

☐ **PRIVATE CASE-BOOK OF AN M.D.,** by Curt S. Wachtel, M.D.
Amazing true case histories which detail cures of the ills of the body through the magic of the mind.   #L92-540, 50¢

☐ **KISSES OF DEATH,** by Henry Kane
The new mystery case of Peter Chambers, "a private eye who uses his brains as well as his body"—*N. Y. Times.*   #90-259, 40¢

☐ **THE WEIRD ONES,** introduced by H. L. Gold
Rare and unforgettable science fiction, by the modern masters of their craft.
                #L92-541, 50¢

☐ **JOHNNY HAVOC MEETS ZELDA,** by John Jakes
The most explosive detective since Mickey Spillane's Mike Hammer. "Really wild"—*N. Y. Times.*   #90-261, 40¢

☐ **ARENA OF LOVE,** by Helene Eliat
The novel of a perverted love affair. Unexpurgated translation from the French.
                #90-262, 40¢

☐ **DOCTORS AND NURSES,** by Virginia McDonnell, R.N.
Forbidden stories about lives in torment . . . true cases from hospital files.
                #90-263, 40¢

☐ **THE STRANGER FROM NEUTRAL STRIP,** by Charles Alden Seltzer
He brought a new kind of six-gun justice. Another western by the master writer.
                #91-264, 35¢

☐ **THE LONELY SEX,** by Estelle H. Ries
Analyzing the problems of the unmarried woman. "Admirable . . . much shrewd comment"—*N. Y. Times.*   #L92-542, 50¢

☐ **A DOCTOR'S PERSONAL FILES,** by Curt S. Wachtel, M.D.
Revealing case histories of men and women from every walk of life.
                #L92-543, 50¢

☐ **A PROFESSIONAL GAMBLER TELLS,** by Mike ("Pitcher") Barron
How to win at races, dice, cards, etc.—by a man who makes his living at it!
                #L92-544, 50¢

☐ **FOR MEN ONLY,** by Beth Brown
The flamboyant best-seller about "The Oldest Profession."   #L92-545, 50¢

☐ **JAILBAIT JUNGLE,** by Wenzell Brown
"A realistic novel of hoodlums who prowl the city streets at night"—*Real Magazine.*   #90-265, 40¢

☐ **TRIPLE CROSS,** by John Roeburt
"Jigger Moran" and the love triangle case. "The underworld has few secrets from him"—*N. Y. Times.*   #90-266, 40¢

☐ **MY FRIEND HENRY MILLER,** by Alfred Perlès
First paperback edition of the $4.00 best-seller about the author of *Tropic of Cancer, Tropic of Capricorn,* etc.   #L92-546, 50¢

☐ **THE X REPORT,** from *Sexology Magazine*
A survey by leading doctors of modern sex patterns and practices among men and women of all ages. (Illustrated.)   #L92-547, 50¢

☐ **FATHERS ARE PARENTS TOO,** by O. Spurgeon English, M.D. & Constance J. Foster
"What Dr. Spock was to mothers, this book is to fathers." "Recommended as a great service"—*Menninger Clinic Bulletin.*   #L92-548, 50¢

☐ **CALORIES, VITAMINS AND COMMON SENSE** by H. Curtis Wood, Jr., M.D.
A nutrition expert's guide to health and happiness: 13th big printing of the amazing little book that can change your life.   #L92-549, 50¢